KB253003

터무니 사랑

A Cock-and-bull Love

부상호 시집

Bu Sang-Ho's Poetry

새미

| 시인의 말

재지 말자
우리 사이랑
터무니없는 일이라 말자
모든 시간은 시작을 위한 것이다
지난 자국들
보잘 것 없어 보여도
디딘 일 그나마 남아있음에
지금껏 아니 왔나 그 걸음에서
그렇게 이제 함께 가다보면,
터무니 있다 아니 할까
우리 살다 간 그 터에
삶의 무늬 새롭게 남게
사랑하고프다

2012년 봄
물건너(濟)고을(州)
쇠귀(牛耳) 부 상 호

차 례 Contents

제2부 내 화분에 옮겨 심다
Chapter 2 Transplanted into My Flowerpot

제3부 아틀라스의 그 화분(花盆)
Chapter 3   The Load of Atlas's Flowerpot

제1부

아니
아픈 꽃

백목련

이렇게 낳으려고
겨우내 그렇게 인고(忍苦)하셨습니까
하늘 끝으로 땅 끝까지
탄생의 첫 소리를
이렇게 새하얗게 내어 놓습니까

잎조차 없이 내고
뭇바람에 흠 받기 싫어하는
그 고결(高潔)에 눈이 부시어
눈이 부시어
외려 뒷걸음이 납니다.

범상(凡常)에 응답하느니 차라리
수명에 연연 않고 홀홀 떠나는
임의 지순(至純)을 압니다
또 한 세상 기다려야 합니까
날은 저물녘 조바심만 커 갑니다

─영역시(英譯詩)는 133쪽에.

달맞이꽃

달 맞으려
피는 꽃이라며
겨울밤 보름달은
홀로 외롭다

그 이름 날 주오
네 철 동그랗게
내 맘 속에 앉은
보름달 당신

— 영역시(英譯詩)는 134쪽에.

나팔꽃

누군가 없으면 어떠랴
그의 저 속뜻 헤아리는
삶이란 저마다 홀 걸음

온 세상 잠 든 새 저 홀로 가는 길
깜깜한 밤새며 손끝 마디 가늠으로
별빛에 길 트는 바지랑대 오직 믿고

한 줄기 불평 없이 이 길을 오르다
탓하랴 어느 누군가 듣는 이 없어도
목청껏 드맑게 새벽 틔우는 저 소리

—영역시(英譯詩)는 135쪽에.

수련(睡蓮)

당신처럼 살게 하소서
땅은 딛고
물에는 흐르며
하늘은 표정에 담아
그렇게 살게 하소서

삶에는 속이 얼마나 깊어야
내색도 않으며
흐르면 흐르고
앉히면 내리고 띄우면 뜨며
그렇게 살게 하소서

그제도 어제도
오늘로 잇고
내일을 맞으며
모든 걸 바탕으로
그냥 그대로 살게 하소서

바람이 이는
동글 또 동글, 동그라미들
아무리 흔들려도 그걸 내며
둥글게 둥글게
그렇게 살게 하소서

진흙을 딛고
물에는 물처럼
곱게 피우려는 염원을
합장으로 간직하고
기도하며 살게 하소서

―영역시(英譯詩)는 136쪽에.

봉숭아

숭아야!
교복 칼라 하얀
누이를 부르고

봉숭아씨!
머리총 길게 땋은
이웃집 처녀
휴가 기다리는 병사
고향 골목 어귀에 핀
미소

헛수작 바람엔
담 밖으로 톡!
내던지는
모성애

어린애 된
우리 어머니
새끼손톱에 이는
소꿉놀이 다듬이
그 소리

참깨꽃

참깨는 하얗게 꽃을 피우면
비탈 밭 뙈기 아침 햇살에
세수를 하는 우리 누이이다

세상은 날씨가 준다
오늘은 어제와 다르고
어제도 그제와 다르게
날은 씨를 뿌리고 있다

꽃을 곱다고만 볼 수 있음은
그렇게 만이면 오죽 좋으랴만
그것은 철부지한 호강 아닌가

함지박 들어야 내 곡식인 걸
담기 바로 전 쏟뜨리는 폭우들
하얗게 고운 만큼 조바심 난다

꽃을 피움은 친정이고
영글음은 시댁 몫인데
이음은 한 결로 참이다

참깨가 하얗게 웃으면
내 안에 날씨는 해맑고
눈길은 먼 데 하늘로 간다

—영역시(英譯詩)는 138쪽에.

석류꽃

볕살은 쨍그렁대고
응달이 잎사귀 스쳐
마루로 살랑 댓돌을 넘다

졸던 부채에 실려
마음까지 녹아내리다
홀연히 시선이 붙들리는 곳

그 눈맞춤
전생이 이은 것인가
낮이 달아올라
시선이 먼 산으로 날았다
되 끌리어 도로 왔을 땐

기다리고 있었다는 듯
더욱 또렷이 쏘아오는
지난 세월 다 모아 펼치며
선명히 들려오는 눈길 소리

한여름 햇살보다
더 뜨겁게 끌어올리는
심연(深淵)에 뿌리 깊은
설렘이라는 그 이름

－영역시(英譯詩)는 140쪽에.

모심꽃

절 옆 오솔길을 산책하다
절 밖 울담 밑 풀꽃 하나
이름도 모르는 그 꽃 함께
눈총 마주친 그게 인연인가
꽃은 사람 더불어 살아가야하고
사람도 꽃마냥 지낼 수 있다면야
잘 키워 줄 테니 우리 집으로 가자
털뿌리 끝 아니 다치게 파 싸고
화분에 곱게 심기어 탄생되었다
어른들 잘 모시라 바라며
형제간엔 도탑게 살라하고
모심꽃이라 지어 줘 불렀었다
군복무 하늬 철을 한데서 잘 보냈고
이런저런 면허들도 취득해 오더니만
홀로서기 아니 될 텐가 그러던 차에
아! 어느 날 밤새 바싹 말라 있었다

품에 그 꽃 묻었던 그 날
그제야 문득 떠오르는 말
그 절 앞을 지나올 그 때
스님이 우연인가 던져 온 말

그 꽃은 절에서나 살아 간다

—영역시(英譯詩)는 142쪽에.

상사화(相思花)

몸 사위어 맘 나고
그 맘 지면 몸이 난다
만날 수 없는 만큼 더 짙은
넋으로나 토해내는 그리운 고함
딛고 선 땅 위에서 스러지기까지
몸과 맘 엇 만남에 건네받은 것은
주지 않는 걸랑 애써 받으려 말자

서로 못 만나는 사바 인연이어도
둘이 하나가 되는 곳이 있다
그곳에 가면 같이 있다
눈에 띄지 않는 그곳
서로 보듬고
땅속에서
뿌리로

—영역시(英譯詩)는 144쪽에.

국화꽃

화분 보듬어 젖 먹이 듯
망울이 옹알이로 보일 때
등 뒤에서 아들 놈 놀다가
구슬치기에 잃은 걸 뺏듯이
줌 가득 꽃망울 따고 있었다

한 송이 맺으려 보낸 계절들
장구채 끝처럼 허공을 저었고
그렇게 그 해는 대궁만 남았다

하얀 국화 더미에 홀로 묻히어
구름 되어 그놈이 향연을 탈 때
손바닥에 쥐었던 망울들 만발하여
이 꽃으로 보십사 돌려주고 갔다

－영역시(英譯詩)는 145쪽에.

패랭이꽃

그 소녀를 닮았다

보리는 익어 가는데
개학 후 나온 날이 더 적은
팔과 다리가 같이 가느다란
글쓰기를 좋아 했었지
별스럽지 않은 일에도
이내 살랑 수줍은 홍조

군에 간 총각 선생
위문편지 끊긴 세월 한 자락에
별이 되었다는 낙엽 소리 잊고
그 바람결 주름 골만 남겨놨지

보리는 익어가고 올해도
색자랑에 마냥 재잘대는
학교 현관 앞 패랭이꽃들

그 소녀를 닮았다

―영역시(英譯詩)는 146쪽에.

들국화

그 날이 올 것이다
사랑한다 말 못해도
이 내 마음 헤아리며
그 말 앞서 꺼내주는

기다리며 기다리다 그 날을
삭이다 안으로 그렇게 홀로
서리철 늦가을 등이 어찌나 시렸는지
바람으로 쏟아내고 하늘로 솟아 오른

짝사랑 모든 영혼들이
향연(香煙) 길 더듬어
길섶에 내려 앉아
별들로 피었나

—영역시(英譯詩)는 147쪽에.

민들레

모질게 샛노랗던 그 시절은
칼 하늬도 외려 포근했었고
길섶 지나다 서 주는 이 없어도
길이야 저마다 바쁜 세상 아닌가

시들지 않음이 어이 꿈이 되겠는가
제삿상에 무릎 꿇듯 대궁 끝 둥글게
풀씨들 낱낱 갈 길에 두 손 모아온
어머니라는 이름에 길디 긴 세상에서

시들고 말라 사위어도 꿈조차 사라질까
남겨진 조상님 말씀 한 마디 안 들렸고
눈 밝혀 찾아본들 남긴 글 한 자 없었던
남매들 오로지 품기어온 끝자락 세상에서

어머니!
치매라는 지우개에
세월 기억 그리도 흩날려갔나
하얗게 매달리던 그 시절 떠올려 드려 봐도
처녀 그 시절 외할배 말씀처럼
풀씨들 자랐다 일러도

돌부처님!
가부좌하시어
어찌 여시려는지 오는 세상을

─영역시(英譯詩)는 148쪽에.

개복숭아

텃밭 멍에엔
봄동 배추꽃
외양간 모퉁이엔
삭풍에 양달로 등 굽은
개복숭아 한 그루

복숭아꽃 한 송이
바람 타 내리는 소릴
병아리도 기웃 살폈다 놓고
세상은 본디 제각각 간다는가
세목(世目)들아 불어라
홀로 피운다

열매를 못 먹으니
불리어도 개복숭아라고
한 알이라도 더 차게 영글려
아픔처럼 부신 외로움 삭이며
후사(後嗣)에 쏟는
저 붉은 넋들

—영역시(英譯詩)는 150쪽에.

제2부

내 화분에 옮겨 심다

차(茶)

베란다를 후드득 후드득
밤비가 콩 방울을 키질한다
칠흑 장막은 옛이야기 속으로
오막 암자(庵子)를 싸 품었다
방문 열면 부엌인 한 칸 오막

노승(老僧)이 되어
찻물을 데핀다
지나는 빗소리 몇 방울 빚어다가
백자(白磁) 차관(茶罐)이 아니어도
이것은 묵상을 바치는 공양이다

차향의 실 한 올 타고
영혼이 불러 내려앉는다
나는 모사(茅沙) 접시이다
풀(草) 사람(人) 나무(木)가 우러난
차(茶)는 말문을 튼다
저 세상까지도

— 영역시(英譯詩)는 153쪽에.

가랑비

학교 풀고 집으로 오는 길목
비가 내린다
가랑비가 내린다

걸음이 가볍다
폴짝, 한 발로 한번
폴짝, 폴짝 다른 발로 두 번

비가 밭일 막아
엄마가 집에 계실테니
엄마가 계실테니
골목 밖 마중 나온 보리 볶는 냄새

우리학교 운동장 잔디가
푸르다, 푸르다
쉰 해가 지난 오늘 아침
가랑비가 보리를 볶는다

무엇을
어떻게 드셨습니까?
오늘은
어머니!

- 영역시(英譯詩)는 154쪽에.

하루

아침에 걸어나서는
공양 찾아 나서는 길

저녁엔 이미 난 길
빈 바랑 딛는 귀가

불 끄고 날
깜깜하게 묻었더니

허수아비 눈에 반짝
길 없는 저 허공에
비쳐 오는 별
하나

―영역시(英譯詩)는 156쪽에.

그 이름

바람에게 물었더니
모른다 설렁 지나가고

참새도
왜 그걸 묻느냐
비웃듯 소리 조각들 남기고

안다고 할 듯 말 듯
흔들다 끝내 말 대신에
나무람만 흔드는 나뭇가지

그런 날
깜깜한 하루이불
덮어서 누웠더니

내 가슴 속 어디에
뭉클뭉클 만져지는
한 이름

ー영역시(英譯詩)는 157쪽에.

부탁

매미야
살려거든 평생을
나에게 이끼 붙어
조용히 있어다오

매미야
네 어미 벗은 허물
그 모습에 그러면
다 삭도록 울어라

매미야
너의 그 울음으로
저곳까지 달랜다하면
널 곡비로 쓰게 하여

두 세상 끝
들리게 해다오

— 영역시(英譯詩)는 158쪽에.

고추잠자리

고추잠자리 한 마리
세월 속을 날고 있다

가을 운동회 그 때에서
책갈피 코스모스 심었던
맘속 그 소녀 머리 위를
휘 돌더니

이젠 별이 된
그 놈이 갑자기
아빠! 쉬!
그 고추 위를
두어 바퀴 돌아오는 순간

할부지 저게 뭐예요
응, 고추잠자리
저거 잡아 주세요
보채는 외손자

―영역시(英譯詩)는 159쪽에.

술잔 속엔

술 못하는 벗에겐
물이 대신해 좋다

'물' 윗부분 빙글 돌려
시계바늘 거꾸로 가면
'말'이 되어 오며 간다

벗이여, 널 찾아 앉아
술처럼 섬기고 물잔을
말 또한 물처럼 따르면

물맛
말맛
술맛
살맛까지

섞여
너와 나
가름들 말자

―영역시(英譯詩)는 160쪽에.

승진

깨비야 깨비야 방아깨비야
절 열 번 꾸벅꾸벅 해 보거라
뒷다리 놓아 날려 보내 주지

먼 산 보고 꾸벅
하늘 보고 땅 보고 또 꾸벅
어제나 오늘도 손 모아 꾸벅

어느 날 지쳤는지 잠자코 있다
잠자지 말고 해야지 등을 흔든다
왠지 꿈적 않고 배만 볼락거린다

눈을 부라리며 절을 하라 다그친다
더듬이가 더듬더듬 노인네 말을 한다
뒷다리 놓아 주오 이미 퇴임 때 되었오

—영역시(英譯詩)는 162쪽에.

존재

반주로 소주를 찾는데
매우 못 마땅한 표정이
아내의 등 뒤에서 보였다

밥맛 얻으려 소주인데
식탁이 이리 싫어하니
굳이 꾸역꾸역 마시랴

이녁대로 반주 없는 식사
소화되며 부아만 부글부글
없이 살거나 따로 산다면

한 노인이 길 바닥에 내 앉아
나 혼자 어떻게 살라고 엉엉
아니나 다를까 그 날 밤 꿈에서

울다보니 깨어
휴! 이마에 식은땀
꿈이었으니 다행이다

—영역시(英譯詩)는 163쪽에.

김장

슬픔은
슬며시 파 들어와
품기어 드는 구덩이
그 속에
푸릇푸릇 노여움을
하늘이 준 선물
눈물로 폭 절여
마음 항아리에 쟁이며
차곡차곡 담아 덮으면,
낮엔 구름이
별들도 밤엔
내 시선 토닥이며
저냥 삭이라 하여,
세월이 꺼내면
그 맛도 새롭게
기쁨이 아니 될까

―영역시(英譯詩)는 165쪽에.

함박눈

눈송이들
어머 어쩌나 어머 어쩌나
흩뿌려 내리니

그 속에
덩달아 마음 조각들도
술래잡기 한다

찾을 듯
잡힐 듯 끌려
어디까지 갈 텐가 흐르다

쫓을 일 없이
다 그냥 놔두고
안으로 들었더니

송이송이 제 각각
닿을 곳은 정해진 그곳이라
모르는 이 하나 없다
이른다

—영역시(英譯詩)는 166쪽에.

인연(因緣)

울 아빠 사모관대에 말 타고
울 엄마 족두리에 가마 타고
얼마나 기분이 좋았었는지
집마당에 들어설 때 보니
어디에서 떨어뜨렸는지
사모 뒷날개 하나
보이지 않더라

첫 친정 나들이 다녀올 때
가마 지났던 고샅길 길섶에
제비 앉은 듯 날갯짓 하며
사모의 그 한 쪽 날개가
꽃 위에 제비나비인가
새색시 두 눈에
또렷이 보이더라

— 영역시(英譯詩)는 167쪽에.

어떤 대화

1
창문 환하여 밖을 보니
차가운 동천에 달이 켜져 있습니다
죄송합니다
밤 새 당신을 밖에 두고
깜빡 잠이 들었습니다
지금
생각을 내려 끄겠습니다

2
생각을 끄려 해도
마음은 한 가운데
달처럼 아니 남을까

밀물에 맞춰오고
썰물에 이울면서
그 말씀 한 마디

당신이라는 부름만이면
이냥 매달려 있겠습니다
동천(冬天)에서 차고 기울며

─영역시(英譯詩)는 168쪽에.

예행(豫行)

학생들과 한라산 산행(山行)이다

여학생을 앞장에서 걷게 하고
남학생이 밀어 주듯 뒤 따른다
예순도 가운데 가는 할배 선생
뒤쳐질까 맨 앞에서
미리 앞서 출발했다

난대림 기슭
여학생들이 추월하며
둥글둥글 궁둥이들만 뒤에 뵈고

온대림에서
남학생 여학생이 잠시 섞였다
한대림 끝자락 닿기 전
이내 장정들에게 뒤쳐지더니

결국
풀포기도 듬성듬성
덧없다 표정 감추는
그 지대에서

홀로 걷는다

-영역시(英譯詩)는 170쪽에.

메시지

미안해 마라
너 먼저 갔다고
그럴수록 흐트러져
바람으로 흐를 수도
구름 되어 아우를 수도
도로 내려 올 수는 더욱
없는 게 아닐 텐가 그 세상

참척(慘慽)이라고 이곳에선
없으니 그리움 더 알고
바람에 고맙다 하기도
구름에 미소 보내고
남 탓으로 않으며
그런 길 걷는다
클릭!

—영역시(英譯詩)는 172쪽에.

방귀

소리로 속을 내보일 때도 있고
코에 닿아 눈치 채기도 하지만
혼자 속 앓는 총각이나 처녀
괜히 하늘인양 으스대거나
땅처럼 내숭으로 뽐내며
알아주길 서로 바라다
아닌 척 꾹 참으려다
몸이 맘 달리 그만
팡파르 내고 마는
초특급 꽃 엽서
아닌가베
참! 무슨

―영역시(英譯詩)는 173쪽에.

구인

사람을 찾아 나섰다
사랑이란 라벨 붙여
내가 누구인지도 모르며
밖으로 마냥 돌아다녔다

사람이면 사랑하는지
사랑이라면 한 결인지
내 맘새부터 모르면서
헤매며 돌아다녔다

그물 새 지나는 바람도
잔물결 너울로 내는 걸
세월 속에 남겨진 그림자도
걸음 내내 따라 다니는 것

모든 불빛을 끄고
어둠 속으로 들어가련다
나로써 생기는 그림자 없는
침묵의 암실로 들어가

사람을 찾습니다
귀 막고 눈 감아
찾습니다
나를

―영역시(英譯詩)는 174쪽에.

제3부

아틀라스의 그 화분(花盆)

국밥 vs 명함

장터 맛은 국밥집
모둠접시 위 모둠처럼
그릇 떠올리며들 모인다

맛소금 비닐 포장 솜씨
순대 속 넣듯 달인이다
맛의 삼원색 두루 섞어온
푸짐으로 손가락 굵어졌다

사람마다 제 맛낼 게 있다 하는데
숟가락만 올렸다 내렸다 할 게 아니라
나도 무엔가 솜씰 내어 보이고 싶어
한자와 영어로 된 명함을 내어주었다

불경 소릴 쇠귀가 투둑 털듯
동전 바구니 너머 튕기어지고
레시피 따윈 어느 나라 말인지
국밥이 굳이 알아서 뭬 하랴, 흥!

글자를 모름으로써 더욱
진국이 보글보글 김 내는
국밥집 골목 모퉁이 나올 때,
하늬가 내려치는 손바닥 소리에

명함 내민 내 뺨
얼얼 달아오른다

그믐달

벗들과 어울려 술 차를 더하다 하다
그 어간에 왼쪽 눈썹이 당겨지는 듯
그믐달이 실눈으로 내려 보고 아니 있나

아내의 저 눈매
건드리면 베일 저 서슬 나게 벼려 놓고
사경(四更)인가 이슬조차 더 차갑게 군다

술잔 속에선 초승달 손목도 잡으려든다나
그믐달이사 펄쩍 올라 귀퉁이에 걸터앉아
죄스런 단조(短調)로 애써 풀어 섞으려 든다

이 손 못 놓아요!
뿌리침에 쿵! 그 소리에
궁둥이가 아파오고 문득 휘 둘러보니

그믐달은 예와 같이 그냥 있는데
그곳에서 떨어져 길섶에 앉아서
나 홀로 그믐달만을 탓하며 있잖은가

무화과

이름과 삶은
날 두고 무엇이 어떻다
세상이 불러대는 것일 뿐
날 낳고서 아버지가 지어 붙여준
반드시 그렇게 같지는 않을 것이다

미혼모 애기라고 해도 좋고
사생아라고 이른들 어떠랴
꽃 피우지 않고 열렸다고
돼지(pig)에 빗대어
피그(fig)로 불린다

흙이 돝거름 빨아먹듯
눈총까지 뺏기며 삼겹살 굽듯
애무하듯 손끝으로 말랑 주무르다
입 안 가득 그렇게 먹었으면 됐지 무슨

꽃 없이 맺은 놈이라든가
따 먹을 그때 그 손가락으로
다 먹고 나서 손가락질들이다

다 그런 것인가 세상은

뭐라 일러도 날 두고
동글동글 달콤하게
다 내어 줄 것이다
영글어 낼 것이다

─영역시(英譯詩)는 179쪽에.

갈라서자

멍석에서 눈 뗀 사이

암탉 한 마리

제 목주머니 가득

볍씨를 쪼아 먹고,

휘어이! 소리에

도망가는 척 피했다가

한 눈 파는 어느 새 또

슬그머니 돌아와 이번엔

큰 것까지 퍼내려 놓으며,

양 발톱 바짝 세워 이젠

지렁이 찾아 흙 긁어내듯

뒷발질로 마구

멍석 밖으로

젖어대고 내흩으며

주인에게 내쏘는 말,

<u>꼬꼬댁 꼬꼬</u>!

그 소리

—영역시(英譯詩)는 181쪽에.

백기(白旗)

8개월이나 걸렸었다
하사관 훈련까지 마치니
군복 속에 꽉 찬 적개심
무엇이든 잡아먹을 것 같다

첫 휴가 나와
동네 형이 위문 술을 산다니
햐! 안주로야 뭐든지 먹겠다며
촉발(觸發)을 소주로 붙여댄다

안주론 새끼손가락 자리돔
접시에 비늘치고 내장도 뺀
머리를 붙여 두는 이유인 즉
어두육미(魚頭肉尾)라나 그러면서

자리돔 말똥하게 까만 눈총으로
어디 차마 날 들어 먹어 보갔는가
고함치듯이 쏘아오는 응전(應戰)
또렷하게 내 양 눈에 박히어 온다

도저히,
군복 하사는
내려놓고 말았다
젓가락을

—영역시(英譯詩)는 182쪽에.

보시(布施)

TV, 라디오 보다 더 목 돋우어
우리 아파트 옆 건천(乾川)에서
개구리들이 방송들 내고 있었다
개골! 개골! 들어들 보소 개개골!

이윽고,
'메아리' 태풍으로 그 모습 내어
삼킬 듯 터져 묻질러 구르는 내
흙탕, 폭포수, 용트림, 저 포효

이튿날,
다시 개울은 예처럼 싹 말랐고
무얼 주려다 다 쓸려들 갔는가
눈엔들 귀로나 마냥 되 살펴도
들어오는 티끌 한 점도 없다

— 영역시(英譯詩)는 184쪽에.

성냥개비

성냥개비라면 내가
갑 안에 가지런히 살며
밖을 기다리는 설렘으로

불리어 나감은 하늘의 뜻
언젠가 한번 사르는 그 길
굳이 나중으로 뒤 물러선들

가늠 못하니 길어진 듯 삶의 시간
외로움은 아니 눅게 차려 입는 옷
만남이란 부싯돌 치는 그 순간으로

사그라짐이 밝힘을 준다면
그래서 남는 재조차 없어도
悟悅! 그 한 꽃불 기대하며

떠날 길 언제가 될지 아는 이 없고
이미 간 이 어디로인지 넌들 알까만
미리 맘 갖추며 있기를 이 갑 속에서

—영역시(英譯詩)는 185쪽에.

묵

묵을 젓가락으로 집는다

성급하게 힘을 줬나 보다
젓가락 짝만 서로 만난다
묵에게 미소를 보내본다
여전히 냉랭한 표정이다

첫사랑이라 하든 말든
아니 왔는가 여태 평생
매일 이냥저냥
살아온 걸음이다
젓가락으로
묵을 먹어야 하듯

설명할 수가 없다
달래어도 안 되고
찔러대면 뚫릴 뿐이다
화를 내보라서 그랬더니
조각으로 흩어지면서도
달라지는 게 없다

아내는
묵이다
숟가락으로 떠 모셔
올려야 한다

—영역시(英譯詩)는 186쪽에.

콩잎

콩잎 쌈에 점심을 먹는다

푸른 냄새가 철 안 들었는지
밥, 된장 그 귀족들과 싸 안겨도
사람 손에 들리는 그것 만에도
고마움커녕 선 푸름만 풍겨낸다

앙!
거럼, 고마워 할 줄 알아야지 야!
콩을 영글어 놓고 네가 죽어도
어차피 그놈도 내게 먹힐 터인 걸

배를 다 채운 후 식탁 아래에
콩잎 하나가 떨어져 있었다
집어서 쓰레기통에 넣는 순간
혼잣말 하는 콩잎 소리 들린다

어휴!
다행이다
사람 입으로 가느니
훨씬 아니 낫나 이곳이

─영역시(英譯詩)는 188쪽에.

고업(苦業)

꿀벌이라는 놈
꽃 하나에만 앉아 사나
붕붕! 달래며 들었다가
언제 봤냐며 다시
날아나간다

벌 한 마리
호박꽃에 들었다
어느 어린 아이
무슨 생각에선지
통꽃잎 둥글게 모아 묶었다

그 벌
그 꽃과 그 속에서만
시들어 마를 때 까지
같이 할 수밖에 삶을

그 아이,
그 벌로 하여 그 후로
예순 너머 어느 울에
지금껏 갇히어 맴돈다

─영역시(英譯詩)는 190쪽에.

안팎

산행엔 지팡일 갖고 갑서
집사람 말엔
맘과 달라도
마마보이이다

비탈이 심한 곳에선
그 지팡이 엄청 고마웠는데
외려 짐이 되었다 평지에선
이제 알겠다
아내와 지팡이는 비슷해서
필요할 때도 있고
귀찮을 때도 있다

큰 진리를 발견한 듯이
일행들에게 자랑스레 떠벌리고는

집에 와서는
그 말과 달리
지팡이 갖고 가라는 그 말
그 덕을 톡톡히 아니 봤나

밖엔 말
안에서 하는 말
영!
딴 판이다

―영역시(英譯詩)는 192쪽에.

표리(表裏)

학교 옆 노인요양원엘
오늘은 특별활동 토요일
학생들 위문공연에 덧붙여 갔습니다

표정 다 시들어 굳은
할머니들 할아버지들 앞
'소양강 처녀' 가락 속에서
손잡고 같이 막춤을 추었습니다
기억 다 놓으신 울 엄마 자꾸만 떠올라
어느 할머니 손 꼭 잡고 마구 추어댔습니다

하늘이 주신 선물
그 눈물 꾹꾹 눌러 참다가
아! 그만 봇물이 터졌습니다
그 물꼬 남 몰래
요양원 화단으로 틀고
애써 태연(泰然)을 내보이며

긴 바늘
작은 바늘
겹쳐서는 토요 정오
바쁘다 오늘도 둘러대며
발걸음은 반대 쪽
마을로 가고 있었습니다

갈대숲에서

바람에 맞출 뿐,
조아려 배(拜) 굽혀 받들고
흥(興)! 예(禮) 갖춰 등 편다

남들이야 뭬라카든
몸 맘 다른 점 없이
한 곬으로 맞추며 산다
하늘 땅, 땅 하늘
천장만장 다 함께
부끄럼 뭬 있나 어우른다

팔짱 낀 연인들,
갈대 숲 거닐며 귀엣말
당신도 내 속 모르고
난들 당신 다 알까마는
한 점도 아니 흔들리며
세월 내내 이렇게 지내자

바람이 그 말
사람들 쉬 내놓는 그 말
지나다 얼핏 듣고서
갈대와 엉켜 살래살래
배꼽들 마냥 쥐어댄다

－영역시(英譯詩)는 194쪽에.

차이(差異)

태풍이 폭발하는 칠흑 밤
옥상 웨엔가 어딘가 뭔가가
텅그르르 돌덩어리 구르듯이
한밤 중 잠결을 휑! 날렸으나

아파트 어느 층 강아지도 짖는데
잠결 붙들려고 마냥 애쓴다 나는

문득 아내의 그 말
징헌 삶 이제 그만 살고
갈라서야재 못 할 게 어딨냐
그 말 섞어가며 담가 온 메주
그 항아린 하마 괜찮지 않을 텐가

장독이 혹 깨지기라도 할 땐
궁시렁 궁시렁!
아내는 옥상으로 가고
늘 그렇듯 꿈결 속 게으르다
나는

—영역시(英譯詩)는 196쪽에.

제4부

어깨에서 잠시 부리고

겨울날 아침

따뜻하지요?
찻잔이 손바닥에게
궁둥이 응석을 피운다
첫 손길 그때처럼 김을 내밀고
다시 살포시 입 맞추려 오른다
내 영혼 못 이긴 듯 덧 실려 간다

수줍게 아침 햇살 한 자락
창틈 새 기웃 엿보다 들킨 듯이
구름 뒤로 슬쩍 볼 붉혀 숨고
겨울날 아침이 목소리 가다듬어
하늘 땅 그리고 네 계절에게
모두 모여라!
하늬로 그 한 마디에

오롯이 손바닥 위엔 찻잔 하나
그 속에 다들 옹기종기 들었다
봄, 여름, 가을, 겨울까지
하늘 그리고 땅 모두들 있다
당신도 그 속에 있다
덩달아 나도 있다

―영역시(英譯詩)는 199쪽에.

봄 메신저

오랜만에 시골 동생 집엘 갔다
겨울 하늘 아직도 서슬 내는데
씨감자 가득 담긴 부대자루들
자동차 적재함이 쏟아 내린다
와르르 쿵!
마당도 놀라 양지쪽 기지개 켠다

이렇게 해야 해요
높은 데서 떨어뜨려야 해요
이럴수록 잠에서 깨어나죠
그냥 때보다 훨씬 싹이 잘 터요
늦잠 자려는 감자에 회초린
이 방법이 가장 낫거든요

감자는 불평이 없다
입 다물어 입춘
누리 속으로 들어
온 누릴
깨운다

— 영역시(英譯詩)는 201쪽에.

겨울 한라산

창문 폭으로 다가 들어
한라산은 겨울에 섰다
볕살도 나설 양 없는 듯
산(山) 입김에 물러 선 아침

파도의 성토 네 계절 동안
움쩍 않고 덤덤히 앉았다가
오늘 이 아침 더 가까이 더
말없이 내 안에 들어 든다

매미처럼 더위 찢는 소리로
눈물 썰어대는 귀뚜라미에서
다물고 안으로 삭이는 바위까지
지나온 그 맘 어이 헤아릴까 하고

말을 줄 듯
말을 들어 줄 듯
앞에 버티어 눌러들으며
그래도 내가 여기, 여기 있다

볕살도 시리다 굽어가고
수염도 상고대로 붙었으나
깨어보면 그 자릴 지켜 섰다
기다린 듯 이 아침 예처럼

한라산이 다가와 서 있다

파도에게

아니 누가 아니라는가
너울너울 내는 널 두고
누가 아니라는가
그리도 달려들며 오는
누가 그 속뜻 없다 하던가

저 멀리 가로줄 하나 에워싸
보이는 건 한갓 그 안이나
하늘과 맞닿고 있으니 너는
네 이웃 그곳 소식 아니 알겠나
그 소식 어이 못 전해오는가

저 놀은 혹시 싣고 오려는가
그렇담 아주 힘차게 오려마
에구메! 오다가 왜 그리 빨리 죽노
떡잎 보니 뭍에 못 올 것 같은
저 녀석은 저리도 연약한데
어허, 그 놈이 옆엔 놈 구슬려
커 가는 저 모습 보소
저놈에게나 기대해 볼거나

무슨 속 썩을 일 맘속에 많다고
못 이룬 한 뭬 그토록 쌓였다고
구르고, 넘어지고, 철벅대며
내 발 밑을 이리도 일없이 두드리나
너희는 등 비빌 뭍이라도 있다마는
내 속에 일고 이는 이 놀들
너울너울 아무리 너울거려도
세상은 얼굴로 사는 것이어서
사시사철 겉으로 내놓지 못하고
미소로 안으로만 삭이는
이 내 속만큼 하랴
이 녀석들아

— 영역시(英譯詩)는 202쪽에.

종업(從業)

바람을 내야 한다 선풍기는
그렇게, 하라는 대로 따른다
제 싫다고 아니 할 수도 없다
불어 보내는 방향도 크기까지
누구나 받은 만큼 내는 것인데
끼니까지 으레 주는 그대로이다

한번은 절호의 기회가 왔다
온몸으로 퍼러렁대며 항변 할
모처럼 그럴 수 있는 때 아닌가
켜져 돌아가는 선풍기
한창 힘을 내는 그 놈을
들고 옮기려고 스위치 오프 않고
그렇게 해 본 적 왜 있지 않습니까
놓칠 수 없다며 대어든다 주인에게
부드등 부드등
나는 뒷덜미 잡혀 끌려가면서도
뭐 하나라도 내 맘대로 하게 하소
말 해 보시오 이거 놓으시고 부드등!

결국,
내려놓은 그곳에서 옴짝도 없이
가부좌하고 내뿜고 있을 뿐이다
예처럼 끊임없이 바람을 낼 뿐이다
반드시 이런 때일수록 아닐 테지만
일 시킨 채 주인이 날 어이 잊었는지
물색없이 나들이 나간 그날이 그날이다

—영역시(英譯詩)는 204쪽에.

할망바당(할머니바다)

소녀는 퐁당!
먼저 바다에 안겨야
시집 갈 나이로 찬다

물길 속
그 깊이만큼 수저 늘고
넓이 따라 자식들 큰다

한 숨길
한 바다 다 마시듯
서천 아니 넘으려 참다, 참다

엄마!
두 세상 새 가르는
숨비소리로 하늘도 꿰오며

물숨에서 세간도 늘려 왔고
파도고랑 깊이 주름 겹쳐도
할머니 소꿉놀이 텃밭처럼
가름 그어 살아온 할망바당

나오지 마십시오
퐁당퐁당 그곳에서
나이 거꾸로 내려
소녀가 될 때까지

―영역시(英譯詩)는 206쪽에.

하도리 저수지

석양이 구름 새 길게 팔을 뻗어
물결 이는 LP 판을 돌리고 있다
태고의 소리가 아득히 들려온다

三神 할망 배꼽 아래 비스듬한 돌 언덕
그 아래로 들면 백중 불알도 오그라든다
할아버지의 할머니인지 손자의 손녀인지를
한 여름 땀띠를 씻는 알몸은 구분이 없다
저수지에 생생히 녹화되어 멱을 감고 있다

조상들 대화 소릴 수저로 떠먹는 저녁 햇살
밥상머리에 들러 앉아 하루를 듣고들 있다
밥 때 쓴 가족회의록인가 그 내용이 들린다
바닷물은 민물더러 싱겁다 빈정대고, 민물은
이제 그만 짜게 굴지 말라며 등을 밀쳐댄다
첫 마을이 나를 보고 이곳을 택했던 것이라고
두 물이 서로 잘 났다고 수면을 으쓱 올리다가
서로 평온을 찾는 그 미소까지도 기록되어 있다

철새들 한 가족인가 내려 앉아
동심원을 펴 돌리며 자맥질한다
노을이 지미봉(地尾峰) 중턱에서 서성이다
봉우리로 올라 초저녁 하늘을 당겨 내린다

수평선도 잦아 지워진 밤
저수지가 마을을 껴안는다
애기를 하나 더 낳겠다면서
찰랑찰랑 남편을 깨우고 있다

청령포[1]에서

할아버지에서 손자로 내림이나
청령포 서강(西江)이 알로 흐름이나
무엇인가 다를 게 어디 있다 하랴
욕심을 버리라고 강은 저리 흐르고
욕심을 벌이려고 사람들은 그리 걷는가

숙부와 조카는 수원(水源)이 같은데
무엇이 그 줄기를 갈라지게 했었는가
땅거미에 마냥 짖으며 짐승은 다가오고
사립짝 닫아걸면 아리게 그리운 엄마 품
그 소릴 빠뜨리지 않고 다 보았다 한다
관음송(觀音松) 팔 휘저어 저리 아니 섰는가

얼어붙은 계절은 강 위로 눈 길을 내고
세월 엮어온 눈길들 그 위를 밝혀 잦다
아니 들려오는가?
열차조차도 산 뒤로 숨어들었다가
그 소나무 듣고 보았다던 그 소릴
뿡! 골짜기 흔들며 내뱉고 있잖은가

---

1) 단종(端宗)이 유배 되었던 곳, 강원도 영월군.

강은 예나 흐르고
세월 덧 바뀌어도
옛 그 소리 예서
들려 아니 오는가

－영역시(英譯詩)는 208쪽에.

월정리(月井里) 역[1]에서

수학여행 길
월정리에 닿다
휴전선으로 철길이 끊긴 마을
이정표는 아직도 살아 있다
남쪽으로 가면 철원
북으로 올라가면
가곡(佳谷) 12Km, 평강 19, 원산 123, 함흥 247,
성진 478, 청진 653, 나진 731
서울과 원산을 잇는 경원선이다

한 학생과
역사(驛舍) 안으로 들어갔다
원산 가는 표 두 장 주세요
개찰문을 지나
승차를 하려는데
'철마는 달리고 싶다'
녹이 슬어 말소리도 못 내고 있다

---

1) 군사분계선 남쪽 철로가 끊긴 마을 역.

선생님 지금 뭐하시는 거예요?
학생의 질문에
꿈에서 깨어났다

―영역시(英譯詩)는 210쪽에.

난초 옆에서

하루도 거르지 않고 난초는
대화를 걸어오고 있지 않은가
분무기로 물방울을 뿌려 받아
이슬로 대롱대롱 대답해오더니
나팔처럼 꽃대궁을 불어냈다

세상은 받기만 하는 게 아니라고
방안 가득 미소 방향(芳香) 채우더니
남모른 갈 길 바쁜 걸 미리 아는지
할머니 주름에서 하늘 뜻 배우라며
온 몸을 쭈글쭈글 말리며 갈치려든다
내 빈 자릴 슬퍼말고 더 푸르러라 하고

무슨 보답을 그리도 꼭 하려 나왔었나
그 짧은 기간 모든 잎사귀 대신하더니
덧없는 삶을 홀로 보여주려 애써왔는가
한 뿌리 잎 가족 다 놔두고 떠나려 하나

마른 꽃대궁 밑동으로 가위가 선다
동관(動棺)을 고요(告謠)로 쓰다듬듯이
하늘과 땅의 예의는 머무르지 않는 것
상여 들어 올리면 갈 곳은 저 유택(幽宅)

꽃대궁 보내고 난 후
남겨진 잎들이 입 모아
더 푸르게 말 걸어온다
잊을 것은 잊어야 한다

벚꽃 아래에서

부시어
눈이 감긴다
시간 조각들 모아 담고서
평! 하늘 가득 팝콘 퍼뜨렸다
솜사탕 구름에 흰 깨고물도 붙었다
하늘 한 자락이 한 입 달라 떼쓰다
외려 시샘으로 조롱하려 달려들려다
바람결로 두 다리 새 불끈 감돌아든다

신부 입장!
그 걸음 사위 꿈 속 모퉁이 돌아
세월 앞으로 다소곳 다가온다
온 세상 부러운 듯 영혼들 하나같이
곁들어 물들어도 좋다 와자한다
그 시절 그 바람 오늘도 보인다
시간 조각들이 들려온다
젖빛 옹알이도 흩날린다

문득
눈이 뜨인다
벚나무 가로수 저 옆길
한 할머니가 밀어 가고 있다
빈 유모차 지팡이 벗 삼아

7월 묵화(墨畵)

쨍그렁! 대장간 메치는
햇살 소리에
소나기 담금질 흙냄새
무럭 퍼져 온다
매미소리 선들바람에
실려 날려가고
누렁이조차 누런 졸음을
늘리고 있다

소나기 윗녘 밭까지에
잠시 머물렀다
돌담을 설렁 맘먹은 듯
넘어 온다
밭이랑 고랑 덮은
고구마 잎들
손사래 젓는 박수소리
그 한 결에
신선처럼 나란히 젖고 있다
우리 아버지 어머니

갈옷 위에 패랭이
아직도 남아 있다
밭 한 가운데 예나
비가 와도 오늘도
서로 외롭지 않게
한 쌍 그렇게 있다

하얗게 바랜 시간 위에
먹물 그림자 두 점
마주 보며 있다

말씀

평생 흙과 사셨다
농부로 사셨다
아예 흙색으로 갈옷이다

먼 밭 보리가 배고픈 걸
마루에 앉아 아신다
우리 아버지

첫 출근하는 아들과
쟁기 지신 아버지
골목 밖까지는
같이 나왔는데

넥타이 정장은
흙색의 갈옷에게
인사를 머뭇거린다

그 속을 왜 모를까
먼저 인사가 건네온다
나는 밭으로 출근할 터
너는 가서 가르쳐라

제5부

아이야 아우야
누이야 벗이여

해 뜬다

고향집 그림자

먼지 뿌옇던 반나절 길 포장되고
마을 우물 메워 주차장도 넓혔는데,
짧아진 읍내에서 샛가지 고샅길로
품어서 키워 나간 애들 이제나 오나
굽은 허리로 눈길 펼쳐 보냈었다

엄니의 보리 볶던 냄새가 골목 밖 마중 오고
지는 해는 나뭇가지에 꿰여 홍시처럼 눌러 간다
담 돌 새에 성기게 드는 석양이
처마 밑으로 숨으려던 거미줄에 흔들린다
물구나무 선 장독대 항아리들
할 말을 참으며 삭이는 듯 입을 다물고
솔가리 몇 바늘이 성깔 바래어 눅어 있다
적막이 낯가림 않고 뒤뜰 구룬비 낙엽을 깨운다

드르륵
열리는 문소리에,
큰놈이냐?
엄니의 기척은 저장된 메아리로 꼬리를 끈다

귀틀 위 먼지가 발자국에 낯을 내는데
굶다, 굶다 벽시계는 눈초릴 내려놓아 있다
부엌 벽 새막이가 노란 짚 혈관을 드러낸다
외양간엔,
멍석 홀로 서 있기에 지친 듯 고개 숙여 있고
일머리 갈치던 고무래가 빠진 이빨을 보인다

어머니를 잘 모셔라
아버지가 남기시는 그 말에
말빚도 못 갚으며 어이 예! 했었을까
나만을 챙기는 일상을
텃밭에서 눌러보시다가
소꿉놀이로 이랑을 추스르며,
나의 무람없음을 달래려는 듯
그림자 홀로 미소로 그느른다

—영역시(英譯詩)는 213쪽에.

연분(緣分)

맷돌로서 한살이 마쳐
흙 속에 뒤집혀 묻히었다
우리학교 연못가에 어찌
부부처럼 저리도 둥그렇게

하늘 아래 돌덩어리 깎아
맷손 달고, 한 쌍 짝 되어
명주 이불 속 고른 숨결에서
거친 자갈 길 수레 소리까지
갈며 먹이던 이승 그 기억들
그 소리로 젖줄 내던 시절들

얼굴 맞보니 하늘과 땅이라며
거친 걸 먹이어도 잔갈아 내고
졸음 쫓는 노래엔 외로움 덧싣고
서로가 벗어나지 말며, 말며 살자
삶이란 매일매일 같이 가는 것
짝 지어 그냥저냥 돌아가는 것
숫놈 배꼽에 옹두리 거시기,
한사코 그걸 그 짝은 죄고 돌았었다

우리학교 연못가에
디딤돌 되어 일을 한다
감추던 곳 민 몸으로 드러낸 건
안팎 짝 구분 없는 곳 저 세상인가
맨손이 내생(來生)까지 일렀었는지
밟히며 미소 머금고
땅이 된 동그라미

—영역시(英譯詩)는 215쪽에.

슬픔과 함께

이게 슬픔이라는 건가 하는 것을
셔츠 주머니에 아침마다 집어넣고
뭉클, 어느 시간이 꺼내어 놓으면
손바닥에 올려놓아 볼 때도 있고
쓰다듬으며 어루만지기도 한다
어딘가 들리는 듯 빗소리에도 놀라
아니 들키려 얼른 도로 집어넣어
태연을 굳이 애쓰며 먼 산을 본다
촉감이 여운 되어 윤을 내고 있다

나무들이 어스름을 피워내고
햇살은 이미 뜸 들어 잦았는데
하루가 지친 발자국을 땅거미에 널 때,
포근한 호롱불이 주는 미소의 기대에
슬픔을 꺼내어 불빛처럼 비추어 주면
슬그머니 기쁨의 색조를 띄기도 한다
슬픔과 기쁨을 가르는 금이 없어선가
낮에는 이놈이 저놈처럼 재잘거리고
밤엔 저놈이 이놈처럼 꿈틀대기도 한다

나는 슬픔과 함께 산다
벗길수록 아픔만 새로워져서
옷으로 입어 그냥 그 안에 앉아 있으면
귀뚜라미가 먼 데서 다가오기도 하고
구름 새 달빛이 팔 벌려 안으려 들고
바삐 걷던 낙엽도 곁으로 맴돌아 든다

ㅡ영역시(英譯詩)는 217쪽에.

종이 파쇄기 앞에서 생각한다

종이 파쇄기 앞에서 생각한다
불란서의 기요틴 집행관이 아닌가, 나는
서슬 퍼런 냉혈 판정관이다

글자들이 백지를 밟아 흔적을 낸 것인데
불온이라며 덩달아 죽임을 당해야 하는가

죄는 짓는 것인가 주는 것인가
열일곱 총각이 구겨놓은 것이라면
사랑한다 쓰려다 만 수줍음이 탓 아닌가
열일곱 총각이 수줍어 구겨놓은 것인가
아니면 볼펜 녀석이 피운 심술 때문인가
붓글씨는 비 온 뒤 맑음을 좋아한다면,
날씨에게 그 죄를 물어야 할 것이다
그도 아닌 결재선의 지시를 따랐을 뿐
그 누명을 덮어 썼을 수도 아니 있겠나

버러러럭! 억울하다는 피의 항변이 짧다
뚝! 연민도 유물도 없다
무소불위(無所不爲) 지폐라도
내 손가락 클릭이면

집행을 정지하라
마패의 호령에도 움찔 않는 냉혈관(冷血官)
그 파쇄기를 지배하고 있다, 나는

그렇게 처단하고서도
아무런 관련이 없다는 듯이
태연함을 챙기려 두 손을 툭툭 털고
창문 폭으로 드는 쪽 하늘을 씽긋 본다
오늘을 먹어 치우는
종이 파쇄기 심장을
아니 갖고 있는가
내가

— 영역시(英譯詩)는 219쪽에.

스카이라운지 소변기에서

어느 호텔 스카이라운지 유리벽 소변기 앞에서
바지 지퍼를 내리고 일을 보려고 내어 놓으면
한 눈에 내 발밑에서 도시 전체가 손바닥만 한데
온 세상 사람들이 꽥! 놀라는 그 소리에 찔끔하며
지나온 옛 얘기들이 하나씩, 한꺼번에 쏟아져 내린다

고함 하나가 쏴! 외쳐댄다
잠결에 눈 비비며 댓돌 위에 네가 오줌을 갈긴 것이지
동생이 한 것으로 거짓말 했었던 것을 폭로 하겠다
고함 둘이 쭉! 뒤 따른다
팬티 장막 속에서 음흉하게 끄덕대던
그 죄 많은 세월들을 온 세상에 다 알리겠다
고함 셋도 좌알! 같이 나선다
개미구멍에 폭포 홍수를 퍼부어
애꿎게 떠내려가는 개미 떼에 쾌재까지 불렀었잖아

그 높은 곳 그 소변기 앞에 서면
고함들이 팔매질하려고 돌멩이들 들고 달려오고
배꼽 아래에서 비롯되었던 모든 죄들이
꿰미에 꿰어 줄줄이 끌리어 올라오면서

갑자기 머리 위 저 높은 곳에서
이젠 별이 된 그 녀석의 고추에서
옛 엽서 소식들처럼 뜨뜻하게 들려온다
내 머리 바로 그 위로
별 하나가 오줌을 누고 있다

—영역시(英譯詩)는 221쪽에.

莊子의 꽃 나들이

벚꽃들이 배꼽 내며,
자지러진 손뼉 소리를 낸다
하늘도 이렇게 벗이 되려는가
마음이 그냥 덩달아 크게 웃었다

마음은 무대
그 한 쪽에서
어쩌면 내년엔 못 올 꽃 마중은 아닐 테지
진단(診斷)이란 어긋날 수도 있다지 않은가
옛 봄 안개가 조연처럼 들었다 퍼져가고
효과음 받으며 주인 태운 소형차 핸들은
다시는 못 올지도 모르는 걸음이라는 걸
내색 않으려 애를 쓴다

벚꽃 다시 와자한 그 계절에
텅 비워진 운전대 오른쪽엔
같이 돌리던 굴렁쇠는 그림자도 떠났고

莊子가 꿈속에서 나비가 되어 이꽃 저꽃으로 날아다니다가 꿈이 깨어 한탄한다 '나비의 꿈속에서 잠시 인간이 되어 있는 건지, 아니면 인간의 꿈속에서 잠시 나비가 되는 것인지'

나비는 나풀나풀 손뼉소리 내고
굴렁쇠는 배꼽 내어 오르내린다
새하얀 꽃잎들 웃음 흩날리고
벗으로 되려나보다 하늘도
내게 살포시 내려앉는다

—영역시(英譯詩)는 223쪽에.

섭씨화씨 부부

텔레비전을 보며, 아내와 나는 서로 참아야 하거나, 서로 베풀고 있다고 관용을 으시댄다 리모콘 선택에서 공식 ($F°=9/5C°+32$)이 저절로 떠오른다 부부라고 등호(=)가 붙었다 같은 기온에서 같이 살면서 눈금 대화가 왜 이렇게 서로 다른가 내가 섭씨로 5°만큼 말하면, 같은 어조(語調)로 부드럽게 응답이 나와야 할 것이다 그래야 공평하다 어찌 9°씩이나 음조가 오르는가 게다가, 덤으로 32는 왜 주는가 0(零)이 죽음이라면, 내가 죽어도 아내가 물려받을 32는 남는다 아내가 0이면 나에게 남는 것은 마이너스뿐이다 양성은 평등인데.... 나는 뉴스 채널을 원한다 뉴스를 놓치면 물정에 둔하고, 수입이 줄 수도 있다며 으름장을 놓아 봐도 막무가내이다 아내는 드라말 눌러놨다 나는 포기한다 등 돌려 칼잠 자세인데, 이놈 나쁜 놈! 흠칠! 날 두고? 드라마 사내는 두 여잘 똑 같이 사랑 할 수 있다고? 그 공식은 어떤 환산인가 드라마가 인생이란다 그렇담, 난 뭔가 한 여자도 내 맘대로 못하면서 아, 지금 이 시각엔 스포츠 실황 중계, 그 것은 드라마가 아니다 예상 밖으로 결말이 나면, 드라마 같다고 하지만 드라마가 아니다 드라마가 아닌 걸 보아야 하는데... 나는 다시 180° 등을 돌렸으나 여전히 칼잠 자세이다 옛 생각에 빠진다 그때는 우리 사이에 호적의 등호

(=)가 붙어 있지 않았었다 둘이 팔짱을 끼면, 9/5씩 바뀌는
게 아니라 1/1씩이었다 지참금 32를 주겠다고 내가 말 한
적도 없었다 언제부터 등식이 이렇게 됐나 참척(慘慽)을 서
평하며, 갑자(甲子)를 돌아든 우리 삶이 더 진한 드라마가
아닌가 리모콘을 움켜쥐어 한참 드라마에 빠져있던 아내
가 눈물을 흘린다 화면 속 저 스토리 때문인가?

둘만이 출연하는 이 방은 촬영 세트이다 아내는 나름대
로 대입(代入)을 하고 있을지도 모른다 그렇기에, 저렇게
눈물을 흘리고 있는 게 아닐까 대사(臺詞)에도 없는 '당신
이 섭씨가 아니라, 내 자신이 섭씨 아닌가요?'

— 영역시(英譯詩)는 225쪽에.

묵 쑤기

어머니가 메밀묵을 쑬 땐 제삿날이다 삼경에 모실 조상님을 마음에 품고, 주걱을 젓는다 가루 낱알들이 주걱을 통하여 어머니 심장의 소리를 듣고, 천천히, 매우 천천히 화답의 조약에 서명한다 새벽 별들이 초롱초롱 우물과 애기를 나눌 때, 두레박 소릴 아니 내며 길어온 물을 쓴다 했었다 멸치젓 비린 내음에도 낱알들이 화를 낸다 했었다

나는 글묵을 쑨다
아무리 쑤어도 나의 문장은 굳어지질 않는다

참척(慘慽)이란 라벨 붙은 향로를 피워, 아케론 강을 건너간 영혼들을 부른다 사전을 향연(香煙)에 쐰다 무야(戊夜)에 받은 물에 사전을 툭툭 턴다 종이에 붙었던 글자들이 메밀가루처럼 쏟아져 내린다 이번엔 뭔가 한 문장 나오겠지 어머니가 주신 기억의 매뉴얼을 펼쳐, 불을 지피고, 주걱을 저어 간다 글자들의 소리가 들린다 멀뚱멀뚱! 아무리 쑤어도 나의 문장은 굳어지질 않는다.

어린애가 된 어머니께 여쭈었다
메밀묵을 쑤어 본 적도 없다면서
손사래는
묵 쑤어 밥 못 먹는다는 뜻인가

쑤렵니다 그래도 묵을
사전도 옆에 차 있습니다
비린 냄샐 합장으로 씻어 파묻고,
두레박줄은 뒤축 들고 올릴 것입니다
밤을 기다려 오경을 뜰 것입니다

향로는 먼저 간 영혼을 부르고
새벽 우물엔 별들을 모아 담고
매일은 기도하며 주걱을 저을 것입니다

—영역시(英譯詩)는 227쪽에.

A Cock-and-bull Love

Bu Sang-Ho's Poetry

| Preface

Let's not measure

Things between us,

Not say they are cock and bull, either.

Time is all for the beginning newly.

The past footprints

Seemingly counting for nothing

'Cause they remain still so far

Here and now we are owed to them.

As they've done up to now so if we go together

Each of cock and bull counts for very much.

In the long run of trail we're stepping

That our new life may be patterned

Let me share a flower of

Love.

Chapter 1

A Healthy-looking Flower

A Yulan

Hoping to give birth this way

All that winter have you hung in there?

From the edge of heaven to that of the earth

The first signal of being born

Are you sounding into this shining white?

Showing up bare without even a leaf

Afraid of getting tinted by the common winds.

That high soul looks so pure-lofty

Causing me to be dazzled

And to step backward rather than to talk to.

Rather than answering to the common guy

Instead of clinging to the length of life,

You're passing away in extreme purity, we know.

Should I wait for you another world of life?

The falling dusk threshes my ears of millet.

—Korean version is to the page, 011.

Chapter 1 A Healthy-looking Flower 133

An Evening Primrose

For viewing the moon

It blooms at night and named so.

Nevertheless, the full moon in winter

Is met by no blossoms.

Give that name to me;

Four seasons in a round shape

Sitting in the heart of my mind

Art but thou, a full moon.

—Korean version is to the page, 012.

A Morning Glory

What matters if viewed by nobody
That takes its mind into account.
Life is it that should walk alone.

On the path alone in all sleeping darkness
Stepping forward with fingertips' navigating
Only relying on a pole led by stars' twinkling.

Climbing up without a word of complaint
Hanging in if nobody is expected to hear
The fanfare awaking the dawn fine clear.

—Korean version is to the page, 013.

A Pond Lily

May I live as you do.

On the earth I do step

On water I shall be flown

As for the sky, absorbing its looks.

May I live as what they are.

How deep in depth life should be

Not expressing it on the face.

Being flown if I were let to flow

Lowered and floated were I in water.

May I live as they get me to do.

Yesterday, the day before, as well

As those days be connected to today,

In that way tomorrow be also anticipated.

For the while of those days gifted to me

May I live for nothing particular to say.

When the wind blows, as it does cause
Rounding waves to be circled on and on
However often I may be worriedly swung
Getting along with them in fine harmonies
So may I lead my life not being noticed.

Placed in mud, may my feet be rooted
Were I in water as water does
The longing to bloom intact
Cherishing it kept in both palms
So may I live in praying.

—Korean version is to the page, 014.

A Sesame Flower

A sesame is, while blooming white,

My sister washing morning hands

In a basin-slope-patch full of light.

A world life is directed by weathers;

As today is different from yesterday

Neither is yesterday the day previous,

So the times seed every different day.

Just saying that a flower is beautiful

If the actuality is same as the apparence

How hopeful, but it is as green as grass.

A crop is not mine until it is harvested;

What rains ruin it at the gate of reaping.

No less than its beauty, it is so agitating.

If blooming is the task of the birth home

And the harvest is for the married family,

The *see-same* flavors the consequentiality.

While a sesame's smiling white as a flower
As much weathers in my mind get so finer,
So my eyes keep stray over the horizon sky.

—Korean version is to the page, 018.

A Pomegranate Flower

The sunlight sounds jangle-scorching.
The shady side blows and grazes by leaves
Over the terrace flaps gently onto the floor.

Being loaded on the sleepy fan
Trying to melt down my mind, suddenly
Snatching my eyes to something over there.

The corresponding of their eyesights
Is reincarnated, if not, what causes it?

That the shyness gets my cheeks blushed
Turns my eyes stray over to the mountain.
Then they feel like coming back to the spot.

When my sight moves back half-round
As if the spot had been expecting me to do so,
It's still gazing more intentionally at me.

Than mid-summer sunlights

More powerfully jangle-scorching

From the abyss of the old memories

Is named the Romance of their puppy days.

—Korean version is to the page, 020.

A Caring Flower

While walking on a path by a temple

A flower by chance came into my sight.

Glancing at each other is our fatal ties;

A flower adds its value in human's sight

Man also does so living together with it.

Let's come home, suggesting a warm care.

Digged out carefully and wrapped in vinyl

The flower was transplanted in a home pot.

Expecting it to respect and attend to elders

And to get along with its siblings, as well

It was named and called a caring flower.

It served the military coldness out of door,

Having obtained sorts of the qualifications.

The moment it is expected to make its way

Alas! All of sudden it was found dried at dawn.

Not until the day it was buried in my heart

Had a word come into my old remembrance;

The moment I took a walk by the temple

A monk gave an broad hint to me that

Only in a temple does the flower live for good.

—Korean version is to the page, 022.

A Magic Lily

Not until the mind goes out does the body come out;
The mind shows up after the body is reduced to ashes.
For the reason that each can't see, much more thickened
Becomes their missing; pouring out into silent shouting.
In the world on which they are stepping until going out
What they are handed over from the fate they can't meet
Is 'Don't expect what is not inherited from the heaven'.

Though they can't meet each other in this suffering world
There is a place where both are unified as a body
Go there and you are getting along with each other
Though it's not visible
Hugging each other
In a bunch of roots
Under the ground.

—Korean version is to the page, 024.

A Chrysanthemum

Sprinkling over it like nursling an infant
Sprouted buds as if a baby were babbling.
My kid, frolicking behind my back, wanting
To make up the losses in the marble plays,
Had picked up the buds full of his hands.

The seasons having been spent for blooming
Trembling by themselves like *janggu*[1] sticks
Had nothing to do as flowers until next year.

Alone under the piles of white chrysanthemum
In the shape of cloud along the incense burning
While that guy was ascending up to the heaven
All the buds in his hands bloomed to the fullest
As if telling me to be satisfied with those flowers.

—Korean version is to the page, 025.

---

1) *janggu* is Korean traditional drum, shape of a hourglass.

A Rainbow Pink

It looks like the girl.

Until the barley is ripening brownish

Few days of the semester she had been present.

Arms and legs were gracile like the flower stems.

She used to like to write composition.

Her pale face, at nothing particular,

Was often immediately flushed softly.

To a single teacher since entering the army

A swirling patch of flowing time brought tidings

Informing why they were quitted in corresponding;

She had been turned of a star in heaven.

Barleys are also ripening this year.

As if showing the rainbow colors off

At the porch of our school is the flower.

It looks like the girl.

—Korean version is to the page, 026.

A Wild Aster

The day will come when
Though not informing of its love
It will be reckoned by nature, or
Each will be understanding of each.

While waiting, and waiting for that day
Soothing the pain of its inner mind by itself
Until the chilliness of the late fall hits the back
Not does it burst out its mind, coming up to heaven.

All the spirits of the unrequited love
Down along the smoke string of the incense
At the edge of the forest trail in this season
Are fully blooming without regret as stars.

—Korean version is to the page, 027.

A Dandelion

The early season harshly bright-yellowed
Is rather felt warm in the sharp-edge wind,
None of the passers-by pays attention to;
Life is in its nature walking their busy roads.

None of the flowers dreams of not wilting;
As if kneeling at memorial rite, around the stalk
Gathered the woolly seeds ready to make its way.

Withering and wilting cannot dissipate a dream for kids.
Though nothing about ancestors' encouraging is heard,
Nothing about their will is found by her caring eyes,
After all for bringing up their descendants is done now.

Mother!
On the edge of your life,
What a dementia has erased all your memory!
The white wooly seeds were gathered around you,
Your father's saying to you before your wedding has come
true.

Stone Buddha!

Sitting with your legs crossed and folded

How shall you open and make your way next world?

—Korean version is to the page, 028.

A Wild Peach

At the fence site of the kitchen garden
The early spring cabbages are blooming.
At the stone wall corner out of the barn
The back bent to the sunny side by winter
But a wild peach hangs in there all alone.

A flake of a peach blossom swirling down
Causes a fine sound in sweet wind to awake
Only a chick to turn its curious glimpse there.
Nobody else is attending to it, nevertheless
A wild peach tree is still there, for what?

Probably 'cause its fruit is uneatable and so
Although it is humbly called a wild peach
Hoping to bear even one more budding fruit
Soothing so much loneness as hiding pains
For the sake of the connecting generations
What red-burning spirits of those blossoms.

—Korean version is to the page, 030.

Chapter 2

Transplanted into My Flowerpot

Tea

Night raindrops on the veranda

Sound like beans are winnowed.

The pitch-dark night leads to a fairy tale;

A hermitage hut is hugged by the darkness

Where a room is opened to a kitchenette.

Cast as an old Buddhist monk

For tea he is heating some water

Made from the sound of raindrops passing by.

This is almsgiving of meditation to heaven.

Along a thread of the aroma

A spirit is called down into the cup.

I am a reed-sprout-sand dish. [1]

A herb, a person and a tree [2] are brewed up.

The tea opens for communication

The gate to the Acheron.

—Korean version is to the page, 033.

---

1) a reed-sprout-sand dish: The spirit is called down on it in the ancestral memorial rite in Korea.

2) A herb, a person and a tree: Tea is 茶 in Chinese, which is deciphered into three; ⁺⁺ (herb), 人(person) and 木(tree).

Drizzle

After school on the way home

It rains.

It drizzles.

The steps are lightly quickened.

Hopping! Once on one leg.

Stepping! Twice on two legs.

The rain keeps her from working on the field

Mom is home.

Mom is surely home.

Roasted barley smells to fetch me to corner.

The lawn of our school ground

Looks green, vivid green.

This morning after five decade years

The drizzle is roasting barley, too.

What

Did you have

For breakfast this morning?

Mom!

—Korean version is to the page, 034.

A Certain Day

Walking out in the morning
Is the way for alms to give myself.

In the evening on the trail
The empty knapsack steps back home.

After switching off me and the day
Burying them under the total darkness,

Onto the eyes of a puppet
Through the void space
Twinkling down is
A star.

—Korean version is to the page, 036.

Who's it?

As I hear tell
Having no idea, the wind recedes away.

A sparrow,
For what I am asking,
Scatters pieces of twittering behind.

Seemingly to answer or not
Swaying for a while in the wind
The branches say 'You are to blame.'

That evening
Blackened out isolated
Lying under the duvet of the day,

At somewhere in my heart
A clot or a lump is echoed
In a name.

—Korean version is to the page, 037.

Asking a Favor

Cicada !
If you want to live lifelong
Formed on me as a lichen
Try to keep quiet, please.

Cicada !
Over the shell your mother cast off
If you want to do so on and on, then
Never stop until it is faded into soil.

Cicada !
Favored by that chirruping of yours
If able to soothe the spirit in Acheron
Hiring you as a funeral crying maid

Chirrup endlessly enough for the ends
Of both worlds to hear and be propitiated.

—Korean version is to the page, 038.

A Red Dragonfly

A red dragonfly is flying

Swirling up and down in the tides of time.

From the days of pupils' fall athletic meeting

Over the bookmark made of a cosmos petal

Hovering over the head of a girl in memory

It circulates around.

Then a star of my son in heaven

Shows up all of sudden in my memory;

Daddy! I gotta go pee-pee.

Over the chili[1] then

It flies around twice or more.

-What's that, grandfather?

-Yeah, it's a dragonfly.

-Let me have it in hand, please.

My daughter's kid grizzles for it.

—Korean version is to the page, 039.

---

1) the chili indicates a kid's penis in Korean, and a red dragonfly is a
red-chili dragonfly in Korean.

In the Glass

Were my friend a teetotaller
Water can be replaced for you.

Turned the upper *mool*[1] quarter-around
To the way of a clock-backward
Then *mal*[2] goes and comes two ways.

While being seated with you, my friend
Serving a water glass like one of *sool*[3]
Filling *mal* as if it were pure water, then

The taste of *mool*
And that of *mal*
Including *sool*
And also, that of *sal*[4]

---

1) *mool* is water in Korean.
2) *mal* is talking in Korean.
3) *sool* is liquor in Korean.
4) *sal* is life in Korean.

All those blended in
You and me together,
Not be discriminated.

—Korean version is to the page, 040.

The Promotion

Hopper! Hopper! Long-headed grasshopper!
Bow and bow to me ten times, and then
I will let you be promoted to fly over away.

Bobbing up and down to
The distant mountain, the sky and the earth
Today like yesterday with its hands pressed.

One day fatigue caused it to be motionless.
Though tapped on the back not to fall asleep
It seems it abandoned the intention of bowing.

With eyes wide and bulging, pressing it to bow;
The antenna says hesitantly in an old man's voice.
-Set me free. It's high time for me to get retired.

—Korean version is to the page, 041.

An Existence

Feeling like *soju*[1] for an appetizer

The deep-rooted face of my wife

Is clearly seen right at her back.

A glass being a good appetizer at times,

The table indeed shows the disapproval,

Then, the stubbornness not be seated with.

A try to coping with a meal without a glass

Has to swallow such complaints all the way;

If getting divorced or managing to live alone.

An old man is let out crying on the roadside.

-How can I make a way of my life by myself?

Surprise, surprise! In his dream that night.

---

1) *soju*: Korean distilled liquor.

The crying awakens him.

Whew! Nightly sweats on his brow.

Thank God! It's but a dream.

—Korean version is to the page, 042.

Gimjang[1]

The feeling of sorrow is a pit for pot,

Who digged unnoticeably in my mind?

Where all spotted green detesting angers

Be pickled enough with the salt of tears

Which's a present gifted from the heaven

In the pot of the mind it be laid stacked;

Then clouds at daytime

And at night the stars

Patting me into my eyesight

Telling to let it flow as it's flown

When the time picks it out ma·ñana

Then it tastes totally new

Expected to be fermented into sweet.

—Korean version is to the page, 043.

---

1) *Gimjang* is an event for making kimchi in large quantities so that it may
be stored and eaten during the winter.

Large Flakes of Snow

Each flake of snow in mass
Saying 'Oh! Dear! Good Heavens!'
Scattered sprinkling down randomly.

In the way of swirling down
Together with it pieces of my mind
Feeling like playing hide-and-seek.

At the gate of seeking
Just before the hide is caught
Flowing and swirling down together with,

It's sour grape
Saying 'let it go'
I turned in indoors.

Finding myself each flake is destined
To go where it's already been trailed.
Nobody doesn't knows it but
Me.

—Korean version is to the page, 044.

The Conjugal Ties

My father in a groom costume on a horse

My mother as a bride in a palanquin

How much happy they must have been

Until the wedding parade got home

Not had they found a cap wing fallen

On the way to the groom's home.

On the way of the bride's first visit home

At the path the palanquin had been carried

A swallow seemed to be flapping its wings

Trying to catch the bride's eyes.

She came nearer and stooped over

Founding it was the cap wing of her groom.

—Korean version is to the page, 045.

A Certain Talking

1

Patting the window through the night

In the cold sky the moon is all alone switched on.

I feel myself to be blamable.

Letting you out in the cold all night

I fell into sleep coldheartedly.

Now that all those there then,

Let me switch off bearing you in mind.

2

Attempting to switch it off on your way

At the center of your mind on its way

It'll be seated like the moon on its own;

Flowing in together with the tides

Ebbing out along with the times,

If warmly cheered by thy addressing

Me 'Thou!', then

That's enough for me to be suspended that high

In the cold sky all alone waxing and waning.

—Korean version is to the page, 046.

A Dummy Walking

On a mountain *Halla*[1]
Trekking together with the students.

Let the girls start in advance
Boys follow as if they were pushing forward.
An elder teacher of mid-sixties
Was given an allowance
For the fear that he may fall behind
To start in the very front.

At the warm-temperature forest
Surpassed by the girls leaving behind.
Into sight are their round and round hips.

At temperature forest region
Temporarily together with boys and girls
Before getting to the cold forest zone
Left behind by the robust youngsters.

---

1) A mountain in Jeju Island, Korea. The second highest in the Korean peninsula.

At last

Blades of grass sparsely here and there

As if saying 'Here today, gone tomorrow.'

At the very region

I walk all by myself.

To where?

—Korean version is to the page, 048.

A Text Message

Don't say you are sorry

For you passed away ahead.

So much the worse it would be;

Flowing along with the wind,

Getting on the clouds in harmony

Are allowed if you feel free light.

Now that you are there in any case

Erase things before the world of Acheron.

The bereavement of my son teaches here;

The loss tells what the absence is like,

Thankfulness to the subtle things of breezes

Sending smiles to the clouds like neighbors.

Not saying the others are to blame

In such way I am managing to do things.

Click!

—Korean version is to the page, 050.

A Fart

Sound reveals its heart at times.

A nose sees how the wind blows.

A lad or a lass agitating alone

Boasting as if he were sky

Or keeping coy is the best girl's

Expecting the opponent to guess those.

Pretending he or she not cares the least

Going on like that in some ways or other.

Body and mind will betray each other

Meanwhile, sounding the fanfare and sending

A superexpress floral postcard.

You don't agree?

Why? Save the mark.

—Korean version is to the page, 051.

Help Wanted

I walked out to find a person
To stick a label in the name of love.
Even not knowing who I am
Wandering around like a whirlwind.

That everyone will love in nature;
All kinds of love are same in name?
Even not answering it to my mind
Roaming here and there all alone.

Winds are not caught by the meshes
Cheering ripples up into heaving seas.
Time flows away; its shadows remain
And follow all the way wherever I go.

Switching off all kinds of lights
I will step into the total darkness
Into the darkroom of the silence
Spo that shadows might not be cast.

I shout for a person.

Plugging my ears, the eyes covered

I come back searching for

One person;

Me.

—Korean version is to the page, 052.

Chapter 3

The Load of Atlas's Flowerpot

A Fig Tree

Is a name named by its life?
What I am called and why so
Is totally by the nature of world.
In such a way as my birth expected
My life shall not exactly going anyhow.

What if she is a single mother or me
Born as a love child, such and such?
This tree gets fruition without blooming
A fig, an innuendo coined from a pig,
Follows me as my name in this world.

Soils get fertilized with pig dunghill.
All glares roast pork belly over a grill.
A fig fingertips twist caressingly now
Is swallowed as you please, what more?

No-blossom-fruit guy is pointed by
The fingers which are used for picking.
The fingers, after used for eating, scorn.

That's the way the mop flops.

Whatever I am invoked
Rolling over and over,
Sweets shall be yielded and
Fruited for good and ever.

—Korean version is to the page, 060.

Let's Break Up

Off the straw mat

The moment his eyes are,

A hen alone

To the fullness of her gizzard

Enjoys pecking and pecking at.

Shoo! At his alarming voice

Pretending to run away seconds.

While seeing off temporarily

She slips back again, this time

Pooping down on the mat of rice,

With the piercing claws of two legs

As if trying to find an earthworm

Backward randomly

Out of the mat

Scratches and spreads the rice

Pattering to her Lord,

Cluck cackle! Cluck cackle!

The voice of her complaint.

—Korean version is to the page, 062.

A White Flag

No less than eight months had been taken
To go through the training for a staff sergeant.
The martial spirit got expanded almost to be flared
Enough for anything hostile to be swallowed soon.

While he was on the first leave
An elder friend suggested a consolatory liquor,
Hoopee! Any eatables is O.K. Hubba-hubba!
As if for triggering, *soju*[1] was promptly ordered.

For a side dish pinky damselfishes were served.
Scaled and guts removed; disarmed on the plate.
Why their heads remain intact not being cut off?
For a saying; a fish tastes best in head parts.

Damselfishes are staring at me in the black eyes;
How can you dare to pick me up with chopsticks?
As if accepting the battle as shriekingly as possible.
Their glares shot back immediately into his eyes.

---

1) *Soju* is a liquor popular in Korea.

Despite himself,

The staff sergeant in the camouflage uniform

Put down on the table

The chopsticks.

—Korean version is to the page, 064.

A Giving Alms

More loudly than TV, or radios
At a dry ditch by my apartment
Frogs are making broadcastings.
Croaking! We're warning. Croaking!

Before long,
A typhoon named 'echo' shows up
As if swallowing all things at once
Muddy-beast-burpings fall roaring.

The following day,
The ditch gets dry again as usual.
Swept away is what of their attempts;
However carefully eyes and ears care for
Nothing of the croaking life remains there.

—Korean version is to the page, 066.

A Matchstick

Were a matchstick if I, in actuality
The box is enough to live evenly with
Looking forward to being called out of.

Heaven selects preemptively which of us.
Burnt into naught is regardless of when;
Wishing to be delayed is of what meaning?

No measuring gets a life seem to be long.
Loneliness is, looked at bright, a wetproof robe
For the fatal ties to be ignited from the flint.

Passing away is, only if yielding brightness to,
Reducing to the naught of ashes consequently
Buddhahood! Expecting to strike only that flare.

Nobody neighbors informing each of when picked
Who knows where they have gone ahead is like?
Do get ready in mind to be called out of this box.

—Korean version is to the page, 067.

Muk[1]

Whenever trying to pick *muk* up with chopsticks
Which are confronted with it, it seems;

In haste or by sheer strength they attempt to
Each stick meets one another vainly dropping it.
Instead of sticks this time smiling is operated.
In spite of those efforts it stays chilly as ever.

Our life starts from whether the first love or not,
Don't you agree we have managed to do so far?
Every day getting on with in some ways or other
Is the actual steps of our life to be honest, isn't it?
Just like we have to do with chopsticks at table
Likewise, what are things different from with *muk*?

---

1) *Muk* is a jelly-like-curd food made of buckwheat, mung beans, or acorns
   from which the starch has been extracted by grinding, steeping, and
   straining.

How to do with it has not been found up to now.

Lullabying turns out to be ineffective for lifting it.

Piercing it with chopsticks, then it just shows hole.

Somebody's advice results in such long faces to it;

Even though it is broken into several pieces

It stays unchanged chilly on the plate.

My wife might as well be

Muk.

With a spoon for lifting

She may well be served on it.

—Korean version is to the page, 068.

A Bean Leaf

While eating a bean-leaf-wrapped rice for lunch,

This green flavor should know how to behave yourself.
Being wrapped with rice and *doenjang*[1] isn't in nobility?
What's better is that you are dealt with on my hand.
Rather than thanks, the herb gives off green thick-smells.

Yum, yum!
Yeah! You should know how to thank, ugh!
After fruiting beans, then you get dry-dead
Unavoidably they are to be eaten as a meal.

Filling his stomach
He found a bean leaf fallen under the table.
He picked it up, putting in a waste box, then
He heard the leaf saying to itself.

---

1) *doenjang*: Korean fermented-soybean paste in Korea.

Whew!
It's much better
Than being in the human body
Here I am in a waste box.

—Korean version is to the page, 070.

A Reincarnated Task

A wasp isn't a guy in nature
Who stays just at one flower.
Buzz, buzzing! Coaxing it first
Once being let into coming in then,
Flies away as if never to see again.
A wasp
Allowed to come in a pumpkin flower.
A certain child nearby,
What caused it to get the idea,
Tying the brim of the flower cup.

That the wasp
Only there in the flower cup
Until the flower wilts and falls
May get along with it lifelong.

On the child

A penalty's been imposed by the *beol*.[1]

Over the sixties in a single fence of home

Henceforth, it has been lingering around.

—Korean version is to the page, 072.

---

1) *beol*: a heteronym; meaning wasp and penalty in Korean.

The Ins and Outs

-Carrying sticks is better when hiking.

To the statement of his wife's

Even if it's opposite to his mind

He is always a mama's boy.

At a steep and rugged slope

Those are much appreciated;

All the more burdensome at flatland.

Now he comes to realize

Wife is similar with a stick;

At a time it is necessary

But it's troublesome at the other.

As if finding a big truth

He bragged it to his fellows.

After getting home

Contrarily to the bragged statement

-What you suggested on the sticks

Was so much appreciated all the way.

The talking outdoors

And that indoors are

Totally

Chalk and cheese.

—Korean version is to the page, 074.

At a Path of Reeds

No more than along with winds
Looking up by bowing at the *bae*[1] order
Heung![2] Decorums be properly observed.

Whatever might be heard of them
In the accordance of mind and body
Well are they getting along in a single mind.
To the heaven, the earth or what else
Along with all those on and on for ever
What not be conceived in the unblemished?

Friends of romance arm in arm
Whispering at a path of reeds;
Both of us can't figure out each other,
Nevertheless, passing their words not
To be of caprice all the way lifelong.

---

1) *bae*: the order to bow in the royal court meeting.
2) *heung*: the order to stand up in the royal court meeting.

That talking often heard in the world

A childlike breeze of wind does hear then

While passing by totally not on purpose.

Not to refrain from splitting their sides

It rolls and swirls over the backs of reeds.

—Korean version is to the page, 078.

A Difference

At a typhoon-exploding-pitch-dark night
Some noises at rooftop or somewhere else
As if stones or something rolling around
Blows away the half sleepiness; awakened.

Even a puppy at a floor of the flat barks at
Though, he's trying to grasp the sleepiness.

All of sudden what he is hit on in mind is
She used to say it's time to quit terrible lives.
Breaking up is much better; it should be.
She used to mix it with lumps of soybean.
Expecting the pots of soybean would be safe.

-If any pot were broken, firmly... get divorced.
Grumbling and muttering by herself
She goes up to the rooftop; contrarily,
Who's enlarging the half-sleepiness as usual
But I?

—Korean version is to the page, 080.

Chapter 4

A While Unloaded

A Winter Morning

Isn't it warm?
To a palm a cup is
Playing the baby with buttocks.
Vapor joining their first hands
Rolls up as if wishing to kiss.
An overwhelming heaves his spirit.

A morning-sunlight lap in shyness
As if caught in the act of peeping
Hinders itself ablush behind the clouds.
A winter morning after clearing its throat
To the heaven, the earth and four seasons
-Let's all get together here in!
Shouts in the north-winter-wind; to it.

A cup of tea intactly alone on a palm

All are assembled in huddles here in it;

Spring, summer, autumn and even winter

Heaven and the earth, all without exception.

Thou art here in it together.

Right along with them I do join.

—Korean version is to the page, 083.

A Spring Messenger

It's been long since I came by to home brother's.

The coldness of winter wind still sharpens the edge.

Sacks of seed potatoes are dumped out of cargo box.

Rumbling! Kaboom! With heavy thuds.

Even the yard's shocked-awakened; stretching itself.

-It should be dealt with this way.

-The higher it falls down from, the more effective.

-That's the why. It buds much more than nothing happens.

-The lie-in should be whipped this way.

-It's overall the best way.

Without the slightest murmuring

With the mouth totally closed

Spring is proclaimed

To the whole world

Ah! By being buried.

—Korean version is to the page, 085.

To the Waves

Why! Who says nope to you?
It's you rounding and waving.
Who is confronting to you in
Your surging forward without
Any inner attempt in the mind?

Fenced with the horizon in the distance
Nothing else is seen but things within it.
However, you're neighboring the heaven
News there wouldn't be heard to you?
Why can't it be carried here along with?

That swell might bear it, so does it seem;
If so, march here as powerfully as possible.
Alas! What causes you to expire on the way?
As the twig's bent, so isn't that to get here?
There that wave seems to tender and frail,
Uh-oh! That guy wangles its way onto
The course of getting bigger and bigger now.
Expecting it to bear the news might be better.

What's so much borne agonizing in mind,

How much regret has accumulated so far,

Rolling, falling down, surging up and splashing

You're beating here beneath my feet, for what?

You get your back scratched against the shore here:

How much the swells of sighs heave up in my mind

Life isn't it that should live for the sake of his face?

Afraid of being exposed to at all seasons of the year

Outer smiling, inner getting it fermented is who?

How you could be understanding of me?

These all dudes of apparence!

—Korean version is to the page, 088.

As an Employee

For making winds a fan is employed.

To make them it follows any directions.

Unpleasant things to do must be done.

As much received so to yield in return;

The output including directions of wind,

Meals as well is based upon the inputs.

A golden opportunity, sent by the heaven,

Able to remonstrate in the whole hot body.

How long it had been waited to be granted.

One day the fan's working with the switch on

At the height of producing powerful winds.

The very fan the employer attempts to carry

With the switch still on for a reason or another.

By any chance have you ever experienced such?

-This heaven-sent chance cannot be missed

Saying to itself, it stands up to the employer firmly.

Rrrroom! Rrrroom!

Though being carried away with the nape grasped

-Let me have my way for a thing minor.

-Let me have it. Get off me! Rrrroom!

As best could,

Where it was placed no slightest counter-arguing

Doing nothing with the lotus position but making

Winds still as it had ever been doing as before.

All these may not happen for the reason I confronted,

But it so happened that the lord forgot to switch off.

When he's set out unreasonably is the very day, today.

—Korean version is to the page, 090.

Chapter 4 A While Unloaded 205

Grandmother's Sea

A lass, splashing!
First hugged by sea
Grows aged to wedding.

Under the sea
The deeper, the more in spoons
The diving width grows the kids.

One big breath is held
As if inhaling the whole sea
Trying not to wade across the Acheron.

Mom!
Discriminating life and death
The big breath shrieks the heaven.

Divings have increased furnishings
Though deep wrinkles fold in waves.
As if playing house in a garden field
The sea is authorized for her livings.

Do not come out of it.

Repeat there splashing!

Lessen the ages down

Until you become a lass.

—Korean version is to the page, 092.

At *Cheongreong-po*[1]

Going down to posterity of his grandson
The flowing down of the *Cheong-river*[2]:
What's the difference between both of them?
The river's saying that greediness be got rid;
Men's are walking so that it may be fulfilled?

Uncle and his nephew are of a same fountainhead;
Nevertheless, what caused them to get branched?
Beasts're howling nearer at dusk to the twig gate,
When which's closed missing Mom sounds more aching.
All those sounds had seen to the finest to a pine-tree
That named *Kwan-eum Pine*[3] shows flailing arms.

---

1) *Cheong-river(Cheongreong-po)*: King Tan-jong of Chosun Dynasty was banished there, Yeong-wol, Korea, and at 16 of age was poisoned ordered by his uncle, King Sejo.
2) Refer to the above, 17).
3) *Kwan-eum Pine: Kwan*(觀) is seeing in Chinese character.
   eum(音) is the sound in Chinese character.
   The tree is a seeing-sound pine.

The frozen season makes *Noon Ghil*[4] on the river

The *Noonghil*[5] weave and knit times in details.

Can't all those be heard here and now?

Even the train there hiding itself behind a mountain is,

Soon after all the stories the pine had seen there then,

Honk! Horning out away that the valleys get trembled.

The river flows as ever

Times pass down as such

With all those, the sounds that time

Can't you hear and see here and now?

—Korean version is to the page, 096.

---

4) *Noon Ghil*: a path on the snow.
5) *Noonghil*: eyesight.

At *Woljeong-ri* Station

On the way of a school excursion
All the students got off at the station of *Woljeong-ri*,
A village the railroad there to north is cut off by DMZ.
Though it's cut dead, the milepost is still alive;
The arrow points *Cheolwon* southward
To north; *Kagok* 12 Km, *Peongkang* 19, *Wonsan* 123,
Hamhung 247, *Seong-jin* 478, *Cheong-jin* 653, *Najin* 731.
The *Geongwon* Line, used to connect Seoul to Wonju.

Holding in hands one of his students
He entered the station old and deserted.
-I want two tickets to *Wonsan*.
After through the punch-ticket gate
He was just bound to get on, then was blocked by
A bulletin board reading; The Iron Horse wants to run!
Rusted and hoarsed, even a statement cannot be uttered.

What are you doing sir, teacher?
By the student's question
He awoke from a dream.

—Korean version is to the page, 098.

Chapter 5

My Children! My Brothers!
My Sisters! My Friends!

The Sun Rises

A Shadow of My Home

The pavement of dust-murky road shortens traffic time.

The space of village well makes spaces for car-parking.

To the shortcut-like country lane from the urban area

Who has been aching for her grown children to come

Used to stretch her back on the tiptoe of expectation?

The smells of Mom's roasting barley fetches me to corner.

The setting sun looks like a shish persimmon with a twig.

The dusk comes loosely ablush through the stone wall,

Then is hung swinging on the spider webs under the eave.

On the backyard platform crocks stand upside down

As if fermenting the speaking pieces in their biting back.

Some needles of pine straw lie with no mettle.

The utter desolation not being shy awakes the backyard

trees.

Rattling.

At the sound of the door-opening

Is it the eldest son?

Mom's presence is sensed in the echoing of a laid-in memory.

Dust on the log frame yields prints in each step.

The wall clock denies its eyes how long famished.

The straw blood vessels of the mud plaster exposed on the kitchen wall.

In the cowshed,

A rolled straw mat bends its head tired of standing alone.

The wooden rake, used to teach work-beginning, is gummy.

Take a good care of your mother.

To the will of the deceased father

How come then he did say 'Yes', only to increase the word debts?

The ways dealing with daily things of his own

She's treating with generosity at the kitchen garden.

While she's playing house of ploughing furrows,

As if willing to say, 'It's OK', to his unfilial life

A shadow alone smiles to smooth his feeling-guilty over.

—Korean version is to the page, 111.

214　A Cock-and-bull Love

A Nuptial Knot

Having lived out their lives as millstones

Now buried on their backs in the soil.

Around the garden pond of our school

With such a round attitude like a couple.

Chiselled of a rock from the ground

Given a handle and matched as a couple.

From the even breath under the silk duvet

To the rough sounds of the pebble road

Altogether with the memories of these lives;

The seasons used be lifelined by the grindings.

Matching facing with heaven and earth,

Roughness is grounded into the fine food.

Singing to shake off sleepiness and loneness

Let's get along with each other well for ever.

Life is keeping up with each other every day;

Going round and around for nothing special.

A gnarl knob of the male protruding navel

Used to be seized by its partner all the time.

Around the garden pond of our school

They work as if they were stepping stones.

The total exposure of the genital parts now

Indicates no distinction in the otherworld, or else?

Who's said of their reincarnation but the handle?

Being stepped on, still keeping smiling in the soil.

—Korean version is to the page, 113.

Along with Sorrow

The very thing what they call sorrow

He puts into his pocket every morning.

Any moment of feeling lumpy takes it out,

Looking at it on the palm what it is like

Stroking and patting it tenderly at times.

Startled at the drizzle as if caught red-handed

He puts it back in pretending nothing happens.

Keeping his calm, he stares into the empty space.

The tactility still lingers and polishes the sorrow.

Dusk spreads out of the thick trees

Sunlights in a while shrink on the dim slope.

Daytime closes leaving footprints to the dusk

Expecting the kerosene lamp to smile warm.

In that light is the sorrow shown on the palm

Furtively it is tinted with joy.

Is it because no line discerns joy and sorrow

At daytime this twitters on behalf of that

That takes the place of this at night, squirming?

I lead the life together with sorrow.

The oftener it's taken off, the newer the pain gets.

While sitting doing nothing in the clothes of sorrow

Crickets in a distance come intimately on and on,

Moonlights through the cloud cracks try to hug me,

The leaves on their busy way swirl down around me.

—Korean version is to the page, 115.

Thinking in Front of a Shredder

While a sheet of paper is shredded I think
As if I were a guillotine executor, weren't I?
Even the blood being coldly sharp-bladed actually.

Letters' stepping leaves the footprints on the paper,
Why it being seditious, confiscated and put to death?

A crime or a sin is committed or given;
Were it crumpled up by a seventeen-old lad
To blame is the shyness that doesn't complete his letter.
Or, the ball-point pencil's petulance might be to; not the paper.
If the handwriting's preference is the fine weather after the rain,
Then the crime should be given to the weathers, not to the paper.
Or else, it might happen on the way of approvals of a paper
Then, it is falsely accused of, isn't it?

Crack-rustling! The fair hearing is too short.

Thud! No mercy or no remains there.

Even the bills of omnipotence

By a single click of my finger

Cannot be stopped in execution.

In the process of the cold-bloody executor

The rule of which is borne in me.

After carrying out that way

Pretending I have nothing to do with it

With nonchalance dusting off the hands

I look at the window-crack sky

Today as usual

With frost.

—Korean version is to the page, 117.

At a Sky-lounge Urinal

At a urinal of a lounge of a skyscraper

When opening the zipper to answer the call

All the city down comes in a palm-size sight.

All the people there 'Yipe!', startling the drain

All the past stories dribble, suddenly pour down.

A story of shouting gurgles out down.

-It was you that had a piss on the foot stone at night

 And put the blame on your youngers; I'll let it on.

Another one gestures to shout, pissing.

-In the tent of your pants how long it's been shaking

 All that black-hearted time; be revealed to the world.

The third joins them, gushing.

-Who did piss and get the ant hole flooded,

 But it should be you, yelling for joy at the innocences?

While standing at the very urinal of that height

Shouts are rushing to me with flinging pebbles.

All the sins sprung from under the bellybotton

Show up in a row clustered as if it were a bunch.

Out of the blue sky high over my head

From the *gochu*[1] faucet of a star of the kid

Are news heard as if it were an old card mailed now.

Right there over my head

A star is making water down here.

—Korean version is to the page, 119.

---

1) *gochu*: the male genital of a baby is nicknamed *gochu* in Korean.

Zhang-tzu's[1] Flower Outing

Cherry blossoms showing off their navels

Are screaming with laughter as if applauding

The heaven seems to be allured and join them.

The deepest mind pops together white laughter.

My mind spreads a stage

From a corner of which slightly

Expecting this outing shall be done again next year.

-A diagnosis sometimes proves to be wrong, doesn't it?

The spring mist of the old memory spreads as a supporting

act.

The wheel of a small car with its owner in the sound effect

Tries not to let it be shown that this outing might be the

last

And shall not be done again next year.

Again in the season of the cherry blossoms' big laughter,

The right seat of the wheel is empty;

Even the shadow of the hoop no more drives in memory.

---

1) *Zhang-tzu*(莊子): a Chinese philosopher like Confucian.

Zhang-tzu flies as a butterfly in a dream from flower to flower, lamenting. 'Whether in a butterfly's dream a human being comes into a temporary existence, or not in a human being's dream a butterfly comes into a temporary existence.'

A butterfly is fluttering making the sounds of hands
The hoop drives up and down with the navel shown
All the white petals spreads the laughter all around
As if becoming good friends with me,
The heaven coming down softly over.

—Korean version is to the page, 121.

A Couple of Centigrade and Fahrenheit

While watching TV, I or my wife has to put up with each other. Or else bragging that each bears and forbears with generosity. In occupying the remote-controller, the formula $(F°=9/5C°+32)$ strikes upon the idea. The equal mark$(=)$ is given because they are a couple. Walking in a life in a formula temperature, why the degrees of talking are so different. If I talk in 5°C, then the response should be same in a soft tone. That's fair. Why does it come back in the upper degree of 9, and that 32 is given to her voice as a complimentary. If 0 is substituted like a death, then after I die, 32 is inherited to her. If 0 is replaced with wife, what's given to me is only minus. Both genders are equal in rights. I want the TV channel to be transferred to news. Hearing no news makes it difficult to keep up with the ways of the world, which is connected the decrease of the income. Saying that, I browbeat. She ignores it obstinately. She presses the number of the soap drama. I give up. I turn back and lie on my side. This guy. What a wrong'un! I flinch! To me? The guy in the drama can share his equal love with two women? From what kind of formula does it result? It is said that a drama is a life. Then, what am I like? Even a woman is not in my control. Alas! It's time for live sports. It's not a drama. If a sports result in unexpectedly, then they say it's like a drama. However, it is not a drama. Non-drama should be watched.... I turn back 180° again, but the posture is still lying on my side. I fall in the old memory. At that time when we were single, there was no equal mark between us in the family register. While walking arm in arm, the conversion rate was not 9/5 but 1/1. I have not said the dowry 32 would be given. From when has the formula been changed this way? Surfing the bereavement during the sexagenary circle is the life of ours. Isn't it a good and real drama? My wife, grasping the remote controller in her hand for quite a while, is shedding tears. Is she moved at the TV story?

This room is a filmset for both of us to appear. Perhaps she has a formula of substitution of her own. It causes her to shed such tears. Saying a dialogue of drama to herself, 'Not you are Centigrade, but I am, ain't I?'

—Korean version is to the page, 123.

Making *Muk*[1]

It's at the deceased ancestor's memorial day when mother makes *muk*. Expecting the ancestor's spirit to come down at midnight, she stirs the rice paddle. The particles of buckwheat flour hear through the paddle the beating sound of her heart. Slowly, very awkwardly, they reciprocate and sign on the treaty. The dawn when the stars are twinkling and limpidly talking with the well should not missed for drawing water, taking care lest the bucket should make a sound. The very water drawn that way should be used for making *muk*. Each particle gets angry with the slightest smell of the brined anchovy. So she used to say.

Muk is buckwheat-flour curd. I am making literary *muk*. However much effort I make, my sentences are thin-loose; not curdy.

Lighting the incense on the censer labeled with bereavement, the spirits having waded across the Acheron are summoned. A dictionary exposed first to the perfume of incense, then is

---

1) Refer to 12).

tapped over the water drawn before the dawn. The letters in the book are struck and fall down like buckwheat flour. This time any kind of sentence is expected to show up, isn't it? Following the manual of my memory mother used to do, a fire is lit, the paddle is stirred. The sounds of the letters are heard. Fizz-bubbling! However long it may be heated and stirred, no sentence seems to go into a curdy state.

When asking kid-memory mother how to do;
-I have never experienced making *muk*,
Which she means in waving hands, it seems,
Or gesturing that *muk* is difficult for a living.

I will do, nevertheless, making *muk*.
A dictionary is lap-belted on the waist.
Joining hands will wash-bury the fishy smell.
The tip-toe-caring standing draws up the bucket.
The pre-dawn through night will be dipped in a pail.

The censer calls together the spirits passed ahead,

In the well of pre-dawn are the stars gathered along,

Each day prays and stirs the paddle until it's curded.

—Korean version is to the page, 125.

Chapter 5 My Children! My Brothers! My Sisters! My Friends!
The Sun Rises 229

대지의 시학, 그 향기의 울림
─부상호 시인의 시세계

양영길 [1]

1. 프롤로그

우리가 딛고 서 있는 대지는 어떤 존재일까. 또 그 대지의 숨결은 어떤 빛깔일까. 하이데거는 "대지는 스스로 감추는 것, 감쌈으로서의 은닉의 구조"라고 하면서 "세계는 대지 없이 결코 존재하지 못한다."라고 했다. 여기서 '감추는 것', '은닉의 구조'라는 말은 시적 은유를 함의하기에 충분할 것 같다. 그러나 깊은 뜻을 갖고 있는 이 말은 '이해의 내던져져 있음'과 '처해 있음'이 배경에 어떤 뜻을 담고 있는가를 생각하지 않으면 안 될 것 같다. "대지는 단적으로 닫혀진 것이 아니라, 스스로 감추는 것이며, 열려 있음 속에 머무르며, 이 열려 있음을 자신 안에 감싸고 있는 그런

---

1) 제주 출생, 문학평론가, 문학박사, 1991년 중앙일보 신춘문예 당선, 시집 『바람의 땅에 서서』, 『가랑이 사이로 굽어보는 세상』, 저서 『한국문학사 어떻게 인식할 것인가』, 『지역문학과 문학사 인식』, 『이론을 뛰어넘는 문학이야기』 등.

은닉하는 것"이라는 것이다. 이러한 대지의 개념에는 시간이 공존하고 있기도 하다. "세계는 대지에 근거하며, 대지는 세계에 의해 두드러진 것"처럼 시간이라는 역사를 함의하고 있는 공간으로써의 대지는 우리의 삶을 담아내는 그릇이기 때문이다.

부상호 시인은 어머니를 빌려 대지를 그려나가고 꽃을 빌려 그 숨결을 표현하고 있다. 이를 통해 소박한 존재론적 시 세계를 사유(思惟)하면서 그 대지에 자기만의 꽃들을 가꾸고 흘러간 시간과 소통을 하고 있다. 어쩌면 삶의 파편같은 꽃들을 뒤돌아보면서 욕심을 내려놓듯 소박하고 순수한 삶의 넓이를 마냥 흩어지는 상념 속에 싹을 틔우고 있다. 일상적이고 자연스런 자기 이해를 바탕으로 해맑은 소박성 속에서 암시적으로 대지의 이야기를 풀어내듯 시인의 사유 세계가 꽃으로 현상(現象)되듯 피어나고 있다.

2. 정서적 대지, 아! 어머니

사람은 누구나 유년기의 순수함에 대한 향수를 갖고 있다. 그래서 삶의 여건이 어려워지거나, 다소 독백의 여유가 생길 때면 으레 고향이 그리워진다. 고향은 어머니의 모태이기도 하지만 어렸을 때의 순수가 살아 숨쉬고 있는 또 다른 '물음'이기도 하다. 고향은 모든 사람들에게 삶의 안식처요, 인간 존재의 근원이기 때문일까. 고향은 우리들의 찌

든 영혼을 정화시켜주며 잃어버린 순수를 되찾아주기에 충분하다. 현대인이 느끼는 고독과 우수를 치유하고 인간적 본성을 회복하는데, 어머니와 같은 고향 모티프보다 더한 것이 있을까 싶다.

부상호 시인은 '어머니'를 빌어 대지의 순수를 타향에게 고향을 그리워하는 시간으로 엮어내고 있다. 근원적 자아에 대한 안타까움이 숨쉬는 대지를 말하고 있는 것이다.

> 학교 풀고 집으로 오는 길목
> 비가 내린다
> 가랑비가 내린다
>
> 걸음이 가볍다
> 폴짝, 한 발로 한번
> 폴짝, 폴짝 다른 발로 두 번
>
> 비가 밭일 막아
> 엄마가 집에 계실 테니
> 엄마가 계실 테니
> 골목 밖 마중 나온 보리 볶는 냄새
>
> 우리 학교 운동장 잔디가
> 푸르다, 푸르다
> 쉰 해가 지난 오늘 아침
> 가랑비가 보리를 볶는다

무엇을
어떻게 드셨습니까?
오늘은
어머니!

―「가랑비」 전문

　‘가랑비’로 치환되는 ‘어머니’ 모습. 어머니는 늘 밭일이나 바닷일을 나가야 하기 때문에 시적자아가 ‘텅 빈’ 집으로 돌아오는 발걸음엔 외로움이 묻어 있었다. 그러다가 비가 오는 날은 학교에서 집으로 오는 길을 ‘보리 볶는 냄새’가 어머니 대신 마중을 나온다. 발걸음이 가볍고 즐겁다. “쉰 해가 지난 오늘 아침” ‘가랑비’ 속에 문득 ‘어머니’가 떠오른다.

　시인에게 ‘어머니’란 시어는 타향에서 고향으로 귀향하는 것과 같은 것이다. 시인은 “숨비소리로 하늘도 꿰오며” “두 세상 새 가르”(「할망바당」)시던 어머니에 대한 회상을 통해 순박함으로서의 고향을 배회하고 있다. 고향적인 것은 현실적 물음을 떠나 텅 빈 혼미를 거쳐 또 다른 시원(時原)에 이르는 길이기도 하다.

먼지 뿌옇던 반나절 길 포장되고
마을 우물 메워 주차장도 넓혔는데,
짧아진 읍내에서 샛가지 고샅길로
품어서 키워 나간 애들 이제나 오나
굽은 허리로 눈길 펼쳐 보냈었다

엄니의 보리 볶던 냄새가 골목 밖 마중 오고
지는 해는 나뭇가지에 꿰여 홍시처럼 눌려 간다
담 돌 새에 성기게 드는 석양이
처마 밑으로 숨으려던 거미줄에 흔들린다
물구나무 선 장독대 항아리들
할 말을 참으며 삭이는 듯 입을 다물고
솔가리 몇 바늘이 성깔 바래어 눅어 있다
적막이 낯가림 않고 뒤뜰 구룬비 낙엽을 깨운다

드르륵
열리는 문소리에
큰놈이냐?
엄니의 기척은 저장된 메아리로 꼬리를 끈다

귀틀 위 먼지가 발자국에 낯을 내는데
굶다, 굶다 벽시계는 눈초릴 내려놓아 있다
부엌 벽 새막이가 노란 짚 혈관을 드러낸다
외양간엔
멍석 홀로 서 있기에 지친 듯 고개 숙여 있고
일머리 갈치던 고무래가 빠진 이빨을 보인다

어머니를 잘 모셔라
아버지가 남기시는 그 말에
말빚도 못 갚으며 어이 '예!' 했었을까
나만을 챙기는 일상을
텃밭에서 눌러보시다가
소꿉놀이로 이랑을 추스르며,
나의 무람없음을 달래려는 듯

그림자 홀로 미소로 그느른다
―「고향집 그림자」 전문

　마당에는 "물구나무 선 장독대 항아리들/ 할 말을 참으며 삭이는 듯 입을 다물고/ 솔가리 몇 바늘이 성깔 바래어 눅어 있"고, 집 안으로 들어오면 "굶다, 굶다 벽시계는 눈초릴 내려놓아 있"고 "부엌 벽 새막이가 노란 짚 혈관을 드러"내고, "외양간엔/ 멍석 홀로 서 있기에 지친 듯 고개 숙여 있고/ 일머리 갈치던 고무래가 빠진 이빨을 보"이는 텅 빈 고향집.

　그 풍경 너머로 보이는 "먼지 뿌옇던 반나절 길", "품어서 키워 나간 애들 이제나 오나/ 굽은 허리로 눈길 펼쳐 보내"고 "보리 볶던 냄새가 골목 밖 마중 오"던 엄마의 모습이 "치매라는 지우개에/ 세월 기억 그리도 흩날려갔나/ 하얗게 매달리던 그 시절 떠올려 드려 봐도"(「민들레」) "기억 다 놓으신 울 엄마"(「표리(表裏)」)와 오버랩 되면서 시인의 고향에 대한 순수한 시원의 물음을 담아내고 있다.

　어머니가 메밀묵을 쑬 땐 제삿날이다 삼경에 모실 조상님을 마음에 품고, 주걱을 젓는다 가루 낱알들이 주걱을 통하여 어머니 심장의 소리를 듣고, 천천히, 매우 천천히 화답의 조약에 서명한다 새벽 별들이 초롱초롱 우물과 얘기를 나눌 때, 두레박 소릴 아니 내며 길어온 물을 쓴다 했었다 멸치젓 비린 내음에도 낱알들이 화를 낸다 했었다

나는 글묵을 쑨다
아무리 쑤어도 나의 문장은 굳어지질 않는다

참척(慘慽)이란 라벨 붙은 향로를 피워, 아케론 강을 건너
간 영혼들을 부른다 사전을 향연(香煙)에 쐰다 무야(戊夜)에
받은 물에 사전을 툭툭 턴다 종이에 붙었던 글자들이 메밀
가루처럼 쏟아져 내린다 이번엔 뭔가 한 문장 나오겠지 어
머니가 주신 기억의 매뉴얼을 펼쳐, 불을 지피고, 주걱을 저
어 간다 글자들의 소리가 들린다 멀뚱멀뚱! 아무리 쑤어도
나의 문장은 굳어지질 않는다.

어린애가 된 어머니께 여쭈었다
메밀묵을 쑤어 본 적도 없다면서
손사래는
묵 쑤어 밥 못 먹는다는 뜻인가

―「묵 쑤기」 부분

글을 쓰는 것을 메밀묵에 치환시켜 어머니가 묵을 쑤기
위한 정성과 견주고 있다. "칼 하늬도 외려 포근했던 그 시
절", "어머니라는 이름에 길디 긴 세상" "남매들 오로지 품
기어온 끝자락"(「민들레」)에서 시인의 넓고 깊은 사유의
지평을 열어 보이고 있다.

이러한 사유는 존재를 향한 시원적 물음으로부터 나오
는 것 같다. '글묵'을 쑤기 위한 물음의 사유를 통해 시적자
아는 "진흙을 딛고/ 물에는 물처럼/ 곱게 피우려는 염원을/
합장으로 간직하고/ 기도하며 살게"(「수련(睡蓮)」)해 달라

는 글밭을 가꾸고 있다. "함지박 들어야 내 곡식"(「참깨꽃」) 인 것처럼 "시들지 않음이 어이 꿈"(「민들레」)의 밭을 일구 겠는가. "한 숨길/ 한 바다 다 마시듯/ 서천 아니 넘으려 참"(「할망바당」)아 오신 어머니처럼 글묵을 쑤고 있다. 바 다보다 더 넓은 세상에서 뭍을 향한 파도의 목마름처럼. 정 신적 위안자로서의 어머니, 구원한 그리움의 정서를 간절 하게 담아내고 있다.

3. 추억의 향기, 정감을 피우는 꽃

꽃은 흘러간 역사적 대지에 심어졌을 때 추억의 향기가 배어 있게 된다. 이 꽃이 화분에 심어지거나 꺾이어 화병에 꽂히었을 때는 이미 대지의 역사를 잃어버리고 현재를 밝 혀주는 고개 숙인 장식품에 지나지 않게 된다. 정신과 혼이 없어진다고나 할까. 그래서 시인은 뿌리 뽑힘을 아파하는 고통을 깊이 감내하지 않으면 안 된다. 시적 은유란 어쩌면 이러한 아픔을 감내해야 하는 넓이와 깊이인지도 모른다. 꽃이 아름답게 보이는 것도 출산의 과정처럼 힘겨운 시간 을 돌아보게 하기 때문이다.

부상호 시인의 시에는 '뒤돌아봄'으로써의 꽃에 대한 표 현이 유난히 많은 것 같다.

숭아야!

교복 칼라 하얀
누이를 부르고

봉숭아씨!
머리총 길게 땋은
이웃집 처녀
휴가 기다리는 병사
고향 골목 어귀에 핀
미소

헛수작 바람엔
담 밖으로 톡!
내던지는
모성애

어린애 된
우리 어머니
새끼손톱에 이는
소꿉놀이 다듬이
그 소리

-「봉숭아」 전문

　‘봉숭아’하면 떠오르는 것 중에 ‘손톱 물 들이기’가 있다.
이는 현재의 소망이 첫눈이 올 때까지 지속되면 첫사랑이
이루어진다는 ‘내다봄’으로써의 꽃의 이미지를 많이 담고
있다. 그러나 시인은 ‘누이’, ‘이웃집 처녀의 미소’, ‘모성애’,
‘소꿉놀이 다듬이’ 소리로 치환시키고 있어 ‘뒤돌아봄’으로

써의 꽃의 이미지를 구축해 내고 있다. 다소 낯설게 치환시
킴으로써 은유의 성질을 잘 살려내고 있다. 시인은 이러한
은유를 통하여 시의 본질에 이르는 통로인 어린 시절과 말
건넴을 시도하고 있다.

시인에게 봉숭아는 그냥 꽃이 아니다. "비탈 반 뙈기 아
침 햇살에/ 세수를 하는 우리 누이"(「참깨꽃」)와 "사립짝
닫아걸면 아리게 그리운 엄마 품"(「청령포에서」)에서 "풀
씨들 낱낱 갈 길에 두 손 모아온/ 어머니라는 이름에 길디
긴 세상"(「민들레」)의 문을 두드리고 있는 것이다.

> 누군가 없으면 어떠랴
> 그의 저 속뜻 헤아리는
> 삶이란 저마다 홀 걸음
>
> 온 세상 잠 든 새 저 홀로 가는 길
> 깜깜한 밤새며 손끝 마디 가늠으로
> 별빛에 길 트는 바지랑대 오직 믿고
>
> 한 줄기 불평 없이 이 길을 오르다
> 탓하랴 어느 누군가 듣는 이 없어도
>
> ―「나팔꽃」 전문

"삶이란 저마다 홀 걸음// 온 세상 잠 든 새 저 홀로 가는
길/ 깜깜한 밤새며 손끝 마디 가늠으로/ 별빛에 길 트는 바지
랑대 오직 믿고// 한 줄기 불평 없이 이 길을 오"른 나팔꽃.

시적자아는 이 꽃에 "차향의 실 한 올 타고/ 영혼이 불려 내려앉"(「차(茶)」)듯 "무슨 속 썩을 일 맘속에 많다고/ 못 이룬한 뭬 그토록 쌓였다고/ 구르고, 넘어지고, 철벅대며"(「파도에게」) 살아온 세상의 인생 역정을 투영하고 있다.

그 "세상은 얼굴로 사는 것이어서/ 사시사철 겉으로 내놓지 못하"(「파도에게」)며 "한 줄기 불평 없이" 걸어온 목마름 세월일 것이다. "매일 이냥저냥/ 살아온 걸음"(「묵」)을 뒤돌아보듯 '안으로만 삭이'며 눈짓과 말건넴 사이에 서서 '미소'를 보내듯 나팔꽃을 피워내고 있다.

이렇게 낳으려고
겨우내 그렇게 인고(忍苦)하셨습니까
하늘 끝으로 땅 끝까지
탄생의 첫 소리를
이렇게 새하얗게 내어 놓습니까

잎조차 없이 내고
뭇바람에 흠 받기 싫어하는
그 고결(高潔)에 눈이 부시어
눈이 부시어
외려 뒷걸음이 납니다.

범상(凡常)에 응답하느니 차라리
수명에 연연 않고 훌훌 떠나는
임의 지순(至純)을 압니다
또 한 세상 기다려야 합니까

날은 저물녘 조바심만 커 갑니다

—「백목련」 전문

우리들의 서술어는 사유에 의해서 거듭된다고 한다. 시적 문법의 서술어를 통해 시인의 삶의 무게를 가늠할 수도 있는 것이다. "주어로서의 자아란 자신의 서술어들을 알면서 갖고 있는 자아"이기 때문이다.

시인의 서술어는 어디에 있을까. 「백목련」에서 시적자아의 서술어는 "인고(忍苦)하셨습니까", "새하얗게 내어 놓습니까", "눈이 부시어", "뒷걸음이 납니다", "홀홀 떠나는", "지순(至純)을 압니다", "기다려야 합니까", "조바심만 커 갑니다"와 같이 '시간의 강물'을 엿볼 수 있게 엮어나가고 있다.

시적 여백을 통해서 삶을 뒤돌아보는 시적자아의 서술어, 그것은 또 다른 시원적 물음을 향한 '내던져져 있음'이기도 하다. 시인의 이러한 존재론적 물음은 시원적 사유로부터 시작하여 또 다른 시원을 향하기도 한다.

부상호 시인에게 꽃은 그리움의 통로이기도 하고, 동화적 추억의 회화이기도 하다. 시인은 잠자고 있던 옛일을 일깨워 꺼져 가는 그리움의 불씨를 되살리기 위해 그림을 그리듯 몽상에 젖어 있다. 자연스럽게 꽃의 꿈이 시적자아의 꿈으로 치환되고 있는 것이다.

4. 에필로그

시인의 시적 세계는 은유로부터 보여지는 것이다. 시인의 표현이 없었다면 보여지지 않는 것으로, 시의 은유 구조는 시인이 새로이 설립된 세계인 대지를 경작하는 과정이기도 하다. 경작의 과정에서 비어 있는, 혹은 비우는 혼미의 과정이 시적 갈등이라 할 것이다. 이를 통하여 '이해의 내던져져 있음'을 그 배경에 머물게 하여 근원적으로 경험된 세계를 만나게 하는 것이다.

부상호 시인은 어머니와 꽃으로 형상화된 또 다른 대지인 고향의 모습을 내놓고 있다. '뒤돌아본다'는 게 아무런 대답도 들을 수 없지만 그 속에 시인만이 설립한 세계를 향한 '물음'을 가득 담아내어 '어머니'를 향한 꽃들을 피워내고 있다. 그 사유의 깊이와 넓이를 통해 삶의 역정의 다양한 모양과 빛깔의 꽃을 피워내고 있는 것이다.

"파도의 성토 네 계절 동안/ 움쩍 않고 덤덤히 앉았다가/ 오늘 이 아침 더 가까이 더/ 말없이 내 안에 들어 든"(「겨울 한라산」)고 있는 산같은 시간을 꽃으로 엮어내고 있다. 그러면서 "바닷물은 민물더러 싱겁다 빈정대고, 민물은/ 이제 그만 짜게 굴지 말라며 등을 밀쳐"내거나 "두 물이 서로 잘 났다고 수면을 으쓱 올리다가/ 서로 평온을 찾는 그 미소까지도 기록"(「하도리 저수지」)되는 '글묵'을 쑤고 있다.

시의 본질에 대한 가장 순수한 시를 하이데거는 '시인이 자연에 대답할 때'라고 한다. '자연은 시간보다 더 오래된 것'이라는 것이다. 그래서일까. 부상호 시인의 시원적(時原的) 사유의 대지에는 온갖 꽃들이 어머니의 얼굴처럼 다정다감하게 피어나고 있었다.*

터무니 사랑

초판 1쇄 인쇄일 | 2012년 6월 4일
초판 1쇄 발행일 | 2012년 6월 5일

지은이　　　　| 부상호
펴낸이　　　　| 정진이
출판이사　　　| 김성달
편집이사　　　| 박지연
책임편집　　　| 이하나
본문편집　　　| 정유진 이원숙 유정현
디자인　　　　| 장정옥 김현경 조수연
마케팅　　　　| 정찬용
영업관리　　　| 김정훈 권준기 정용현 천수정
인쇄처　　　　| 월드문화사
펴낸곳　　　　| 새미
　　　　　　　　등록일 2005 03 14 제25100-2009-8호
　　　　　　　　서울시 강동구 성내동 447-11 현영빌딩 2층
　　　　　　　　Tel 442-4623 Fax 442-4625
　　　　　　　　www.kookhak.co.kr
　　　　　　　　kookhak2001@hanmail.net

ISBN　　　　 | 978-89-5628-600-6 *04800
가격　　　　　| 13,000원